Cell-out

Peter Armstrong

First published 2008

This paperback edition published in 2009 by Lulu

1 3 5 7 9 10 8 6 4 2

Copyright © Peter Armstrong 2008

The right of Peter Armstrong to be identified as the author of this work has been asserted by him in accordance with the Copyright, Designs and Patents Act 1988.

This novel is a work of fiction. Names and characters are the product of the author's imagination and any resemblance to actual persons, living or dead is entirely coincidental.

All rights reserved. No part of this publication may be reproduced, stored in a retrieval system, or transmitted, in any form or by any means, electronic, mechanical, photocopying, recording or otherwise, without the prior permission of the copyright owner.

ISBN 978-1-4092-2807-3

Acknowledgements

This book is based round a relatively unknown hobby called geocaching, which is basically a treasure hunt using GPS devices, with optional puzzles thrown in along the way. As you will discover in the book, this is a worldwide hobby with thousands of cachers getting out and visiting beautiful parts of the world whilst looking for a silly little plastic box with a logbook and pencil in it! I have personally geocached in countries all round the world and hence discovered fascinating places, which I would otherwise never have known existed.

I have spent many evenings and weekends trying to solve the puzzles set by the very active geocaching community round where I live, and this book is dedicated to those local experts, who gave me the inspiration to put this book together. The caches, which feature in the book, do really exist. You can find their details on www.geocaching.com, and you can go and try and find them if you so desire.

The inspiration for the fuel cell idea in the plot came from my brother, who used to work for a major petrochemical company in the fuels division. Little did he know that a casual conversation one evening about the replacement for the internal combustion engine had got me thinking long and hard. Any mistakes on the technology side are entirely mine.

Finally, my thanks must go to my family and friends. They kindly let me blend a few small pieces of fact with an enormous amount of fiction. My special thanks go to my wife, who allowed me to make the Professor's wife an unpleasant character in the book, which could not be further from the truth in real life.

Prologue

He had unfortunately been forced to leave America, as the law enforcement agencies were beginning to get way too close for comfort. The thought of facing a murder rap did not appeal at all, even if he was convinced that the stupid little punk had had it coming. So he gathered together his team, called in a couple of favours and they now found themselves in the UK.

They had been here for a few months, getting acclimated, as they would say, or acclimatised, as the Brits would say. Driving on the wrong side of the road was no longer as strange as when they had started. They just had to watch out when they had been filling up with gas, or petrol as they had learned to call it, that they didn't drive out on the wrong side of the road. The people spoke funny, and the beer was warm and flat, but they were gradually blending in.

They were all ex-army, so they liked code names, and the one they had chosen for this operation was 'Ransack', although the plan was for a walk rather than a run. The phone call had confirmed that the family was away for several days, so time was fortunately not an issue. If you skulked round looking like thieves, people tended to be suspicious, but if you brazenly declared who you were, most people didn't interfere. So they had added the water company's logo to the sides of the van and parked in the drive. They had also lifted a couple of drain covers and had a cover story prepared for anyone who became too interested.

The Ransack team leader was a brute in every sense of the word. Not only was his name Brutus, and hence his obvious nickname, he was built like a heavyweight boxer – 6 feet 3 inches tall, solid muscle, and a rigorous workout routine every day in the gym. Actually he looked like a very well dressed heavyweight boxer normally. Brutus, like many African Americans, was very particular about his clothes and had always ensured his uniform was immaculate. Nowadays, he spent large amounts of his spare cash on designer suits and extremely expensive shoes.

Behind the fine exterior, however, lurked a psychopathic killer, who liked things to go exactly as he had planned them. Once he had set a train of events in order, he loved to see them go through and hated any deviation from his carefully crafted running order. That probably explained his frustration with his time in the military, where there always seemed to be a SNAFU in every operation, but that is where he had ironically developed his love of meticulous planning. He had an exact order of events laid out for this operation and could see no immediate problems on the horizon.

He had parted ways with the Special Forces due to his unfortunate taste for inflicting unnecessary pain upon his captives. He had served a stint in an army gaol, when he had disagreed too physically with the *fuckwit* Lieutenant in charge of his platoon, and would have killed him if his comrades hadn't pulled him off. In one of those strange twists of fate, that is where he had met the other two members of his team. Ransack One's real name was Chuck Wendel, who was only five foot six tall, but could climb up almost anything and squeeze through the smallest of openings. Short, but deceptively strong, since leaving the Army he had added to his income by becoming a very successful burglar, as he was also a master lock picker, who liked to spend his spare time taking the latest locks apart so that he could understand their inner workings and refine his techniques. Brutus had made him grow his hair so as not to look so obviously ex-military, but he had failed miserably in attempting to stop his *favourite little honky* from smoking, a habit which Brutus detested.

The final member of the team, Howard Johnson (a name that had caused him problems all his life), was the electronics genius. Six feet tall, razor-thin, and growing a rather sad looking little goatee, he spent his whole time surrounded by pieces of strange equipment, and was never happier than when he was cobbling together some new invention. Booby traps and explosions that looked like accidents were his particular favourites. He spent hours having unintelligible conversations with people about motherboards, encryption algorithms, surveillance equipment and such like. He and Chuck, who had christened him *fungus face*, had teamed up with Brutus for a simple penetration job, as the combination of the two of them could break into most houses with ease. The team had gelled efficiently, and they now worked a regular contract for one of Brutus's contacts.

On this mission, they had brought one of the boffins with them, an English nerd called Douglas, who knew PCs inside out and backwards and thought most hackers were of a way lower IQ than himself. He was also very knowledgeable in the same area of expertise as the owner of the house, which is why he had been brought along on this mission. Normally there was no way he would have been involved in a field operation, but the boss was looking for rapid results, and Hojo was ecstatic to have someone who understood what he was talking about.

*

Chuck scoped out the rear of the house looking for the easiest point of entry, and selected the rear door to the garage as it had no double glazing. A quick run around with the glass cutter let them get at the key inside, and they were in. It never ceased to amaze him how many people thought glass was an effective barrier.

They had been told to effect entry and let Douglas search through any computerised material or investigate anything that looked like some interesting new device being put together. The garage was checked out in minutes – nothing interesting at all. One car was missing as expected, and they had a look through the other one, but it only contained golf clubs and shoes. There was a locked door to the main part of the house, but a couple of minutes later Chuck had picked that. The burglar alarm started beeping as expected. Hojo ran in and attacked the control panel with one of his special gizmos and the beeping stopped. The team heaved a collective sigh of relief and knew they had now had several hours before they had to leave. They had got Douglas in, now he could go to work.

The three members of the Ransack team worked their way methodically through the rooms, finding and eliminating material for Douglas to examine. The laboratory was surprisingly empty and there were no papers, USB sticks, CDs or similar as it appeared to have been cleaned out recently.

The family room had a standard PC, which they simply unplugged and stowed ready to take with them. The study on the other hand had two PCs – one a modern Dell and the other an ancient Atari. The Atari was a simple proposition; just turn it on and all its secrets were revealed, namely that the Professor used it for his music hobby – there didn't appear to be anything of interest to the team there, just a load of MIDI files, but they took it anyway. The Dell on the other hand was a much more interesting proposition and the team took it with them as well, so that Douglas could check them both out in peace and quiet later.

'Ransack Leader, I've found a safe, and it will take me too long to crack it open,' came Chuck's voice in his ear.

'Where?'

'Hidden in a cupboard under the stairs,' came the reply.

'Big?'

'No, just a small household model.'

'Can you extract it?'

There was short pause, and he could hear poking and puffing through the earpiece.

'Yes, with a bit of work.'

'Do it, we'll take it with us. Come back to me if you have problems and we'll let Hojo look at it.'

Meanwhile in the lounge Hojo was passing DVDs to Douglas to check out on his portable DVD player. Fortunately the family had very few and the check was over rapidly with a shake of the head. The bedrooms – master bedroom with en-suite, son's bedroom (neat and tidy with posters of voluptuous pop-stars and Formula One cars), daughter's bedroom (looked as if they had already ransacked it before they walked in) revealed nothing of interest.

They had been told to make it look like a professional robbery, so they also took the silver, the DVD player, the stereo, an expensive digital SLR and a few other select items. They also took all the CDs and DVDs anyway as they could always check them further in peace and quiet. Nothing too large though as they had to smuggle stuff into the van and didn't want the neighbours spotting a group of people carting large-screen TVs round the house. The fact that the daughter's bedroom looked like it had been burgled already would all add to the confusion when the police came looking.

'Status?'

'Two minutes,' came from Ransack One.

'Everything stacked ready to go,' from Ransack Two looking at Douglas for confirmation.

'OK, I'm done here. I'll come down and help carry the stuff out. Hojo, have you planted the device?'

'Just placing it now,' came the reply from Hojo, who sent Douglas downstairs so he couldn't see what he was doing, and then placed a small plastic explosive device in the study. Part of the Brutus plan was for the owner of the house to get a very nasty and fatal surprise the next time he played his piano.

And so the team quietly loaded their booty into the van and drove off. The only neighbour who had noticed anything at all had simply assumed that they had a problem with the drains. They had done the tricky part, now Douglas and the boffins had to analyse what they had found and see if they had come up with gold.

Part 1 – The kill

Chapter 1

Professor Harold Fenwick and his wife Gudrun lived in the leafy suburbs of Surrey. Far enough away from the hustle and bustle of London, so that they could enjoy the countryside, but not so remote that they felt cut off from civilisation. The Professor loved to tinker with new ideas and had converted part of the downstairs of the house into a working laboratory, where he could try out new inventions and prototypes.

Fortunately he wasn't quite as mad as he liked to pretend he was, and had in fact over the years come up with several extremely useful gadgets. The money that came in from those now allowed him to work the hours he wanted, and not have to go through the tedious slog of driving round the M25 motorway to what used to be the office. The world's largest car-park is what they jokingly called it, and he didn't miss it one bit. The only time he used it nowadays was to travel to Heathrow or Gatwick to fly off to some conference or other, which he tried to avoid if he could, because he liked to keep his carbon footprint as small as possible.

Airports weren't high on his list of favourite places either. In the Professor's humble opinion, anyone who liked travel didn't do enough, or they had a private jet. Planes appeared to be designed for people with no legs and airports were full of imbeciles, who spent most of their lives getting in his way. Security and immigration were admittedly vital, but as far as he was concerned they seemed to go out of their way to be as inefficient as possible.

His number one complaint was travelling to America, where he had to give all his personal and travel information in advance, fill in a form giving all the same information again, and then stand in a queue for an hour waiting to give them that same information yet again. Chronic. Every time he went there they took his fingerprints and photographed him. He wondered if they ever compared the latest prints with previous ones, or whether they were simply stored away somewhere, because then it made them look as if they were doing something in the global fight against terrorism.

In fact, he would have been perfectly happy to have a chip implanted in his body that got scanned as he walked through Immigration, but he was also sure that what he saw as the incredibly tedious Human Rights and Civil Liberties morons would scupper any plans like that. Heaven forbid that the 'Elf and Safety idiots would find out about it – they seemed to be intent on ruining any fun anyone could derive from life as far as he could make out.

His favourite book recently had been *The Dangerous Book for Boys*, written by a couple of men, who yearned for the days of their youth when falling out of trees or careening madly down a hill in a soapbox with no brakes was considered an essential part of growing up. The Professor would read headlines about banning conkers, or stopping teachers from sticking a plaster on a child's cut and he would almost scream out loud with frustration.

He had had his retina scanned for the new IRIS system at Heathrow and Gatwick, but the machines were so slow and the average member of the public so useless at operating them that he had pretty much given up using them. He could have designed them a system that was infinitely more efficient, but no-one appeared to be interested in ideas for making the passengers' lives easier. Interestingly he had met the man behind Toronto Airport at a conference in America, and they shared a lot of the same thoughts. The airport designer had recognised the wave of dissatisfaction that was rising up from passengers travelling to America due to their dislike of the immigration process, so he was trying to make Toronto a more attractive place to fly into.

The Professor only wished that more people would think of the customer and whether they were happy or not, rather than coming out with some piece of technology that was fascinating but ultimately useless. No, the Professor was driven by designing things that would truly make peoples' lives easier, or would help save the planet. Even better when he could combine the two.

Unfortunately he also found his fellow travellers particularly troublesome. The number of times someone had barged in front of him at the baggage belt without so much as an *excuse me* was beyond belief, and the way people stood smack in the middle of the arrivals area with their three trolleys and eighty-seven relations was enough to make him spit. He was probably the only person in the world, who liked the new rule of restricted hand-baggage, as that at least meant he wasn't stuck behind some mindless idiot in the plane, who was complaining that he/she couldn't get their eighteen pieces of hand-baggage in the overhead locker. 'Check the bloody stuff in', he would frequently suggest – one of the joys of getting older he found was that you could tell people what you thought! He had written an article on his blog recently, where he wanted to start a campaign called EMPTYS – Excuse Me, Please, Thank You, Sorry – words that seemed to be going out of fashion, much to his concern and disgust.

There was an article in the papers that he had read recently that suggested that they would soon allow mobile phones on planes, which to him was pretty much the definition of hell – being stuck next to some half-wit talking loudly down his mobile phone for hours. There was a second article saying that people apparently suffered from Nomophobia – the fear of not having your mobile turned on – which in the Professor's opinion simply proved that they needed to get a life. The best investment he had ever made was a pair of noise-cancelling headphones. British businessmen at least realised that talking to your neighbour on the plane was a definite no, but some nations, especially the Americans, seemed to think that striking up a conversation was the correct way to pass the time. Sorry, out with the headphones was his first move when forced to travel on a plane.

He had also come to the conclusion that you couldn't get a decent cup of tea once you passed Calais. No, travel was not his idea of fun.

*

The money he had made from his inventions though had one other attraction, namely that he could work the hours he liked and indulge his hobbies. Upstairs he had a study with a couple of PCs in it, one of which was used exclusively for making music. In fact he had two guitars, four synthesizers and a couple of keyboards, all of which enabled him to make satisfyingly large amounts of noise. His wife would shout at him to put his headphones on, but she didn't understand that it was having the walls round you shake that was half the fun. Fortunately they lived in a detached house, so the neighbours didn't get to hear his compositions, or the mess he made of the latest song he was learning. His greatest fun recently had been playing with a friend's group at a Christmas gig they had been doing, as the regular keyboard player had been unavailable.

The other PC was devoted predominantly to his photography. Apart from taking lots of photos, he was also scanning in every negative and slide he had ever taken. A colleague had been burgled a couple of years ago and had lost every single photo of his children as the thieves had taken the PC with them, so the Professor was creating a copy of everything he had and storing a backup copy in the fireproof safe they had at home.

If nothing else, the Professor was always a completist in things he undertook. He liked to have everything in its place. For instance, all his CDs were in alphabetical order, a fact that made his daughter Angela raise her eyebrows in wonder. Her method of filing was to simply dump everything on the floor of her bedroom. He would knock on her door and in a quiet voice ask if she happened to have seen this or that CD, and within a few seconds it would be extracted from a seemingly random pile of junk on the floor - a fact that never ceased to annoy him intensely. He had a filing system and could find things easily. She had chaos and still could find things easily, and somehow that just didn't seem to be fair. One of the projects he had at the back of his mind was to design a new cataloguing and indexing system based on chaos theory, but he hadn't got round to it yet. At least his son, John, had inherited neatness and order. His room was navigable. The occasional unpleasant looking object lying on the floor that had been ignored for too long, but otherwise reasonable. His wife would tease him about his neatness and sorting, but she knew he could find important documents whenever they were needed, and she loved having all the old photographs as the screen-saver on the PC in the family room.

The new hobby that he had taken up last Christmas was a strange thing called geocaching. A friend of his had introduced it to him a few months before, and basically it was like treasure hunting with a GPS receiver. A few years back the accuracy of GPS devices had improved dramatically; his friend believed that the American military had always had accurate positioning, but they only let it loose on the public later. The result of all that was that a chap in the US had hidden a small cache and published the coordinates on the Internet. Lo and behold, a couple of days later two people had already found it. From that had grown a worldwide hobby with over half a million caches hidden round the world, including obscure places like Antarctica. The caches weren't really treasure, they were simply plastic boxes with a logbook and pencil in them so that you could prove you had found them, but the searching was fun, and they tended to be hidden in places that were interesting or picturesque or both.

So the Professor's wife had bought him a hand-held GPS device for Christmas, and they now went off regularly for long walks in the countryside, interspersed with finding a cache or two and usually ending up at a nice pub. His wife was ecstatic as she loved walking, but the Professor had never been that keen on walking with no destination or reason. That had all changed with the GPS device, as *walks now had a purpose*.

The good news was that his latest project, which

was probably the most important thing he had ever worked on in his life, was now wound up. The Professor was a total zealot on the subject of saving the planet, and had been working for years on a device, which would contribute enormously to the welfare of the planet, thereby dramatically reducing the hideous things that people were doing to the world they lived in.

He had packed up the prototype and a USB stick with all the data files and shipped it off to his lawyers, and he had spoken to the organisers of the London Eco-conference to book a speaking slot at the end of the month. They were a bit put out that he refused to tell them the topic of his talk, but he had promised them it would be of significant interest to every attendee, and his reputation as a speaker and his track-record with the organisers was enough to sway them. If they only knew, he thought to himself, exactly what I have lined up for them, they would be screaming for me to come and present my work. But no, this was one invention that was going to be announced to the world at his choice of time and place and there would be no leaks to the press or the media beforehand. He had a very clear vision of how his invention was going to benefit the planet and nothing was going to interrupt that. Once that was done, he firmly intended to stop work and devote a lot more time to his hobbies, especially golf. He was determined to get down to a single-figure handicap.

In the meantime, having at last got round to cleaning up his lab and chucking away loads of junk he no longer needed, he had decided to take his wife and children away for a short break to celebrate the end of years of work, his daughter's success with her A-levels plus acceptance at University, and his son's ten GCSEs. He had wanted to go up to the Lake District and trace back his family roots for years, but never got round to it. He had looked to see if there were any convenient caches they could slot in whilst they were there and it was no surprise that such beautiful countryside should have several that they could go and look for.

He had also taken the opportunity to speak to their old neighbours and best friends, the Bartons, who now lived in Cheshire and they had arranged to stop off there for a couple of nights on the way up. Their son Jake and his two kids had grown up in one another's houses, and Bill Barton had been a true saviour in the early days. His sponsorship of a couple of the Professor's early ideas had been the start of a long and financially rewarding friendship. It would be good to chew the fat with Bill, although he was going to find it awkward not talking about his latest invention, but that just simply had to remain secret till the Conference.

Never mind, he realised that he could at least chat to him about some of the other things he was thinking about at present. He wondered if Bill would agree with him that drugs should simply be legalised, and hence get rid of the money in the system. He had always thought the current system was like prohibition in the US – ban something and you immediately bring money and gangsters into it. He had just read an interesting book on the subject by Ben Elton of all people, and it had got him thinking. Yes, there were several topics he wanted to bounce off Bill, who had always been a voice of reason and sanity when the Professor went off on some of his rants.

Chapter 2

NO more school!! I couldn't quite believe it, but I had finally got there and I had the grades I needed in my 'A' levels to go to Canterbury and study German. Mum is German and we speak German at home as well as English, so it seemed daft not to exploit my home advantage! I had toyed with doing a gap year and backpacking my way round Thailand, Australia, New Zealand and the South Pacific, but the course at Uni involves a practical year living in Germany, so I've gone for that option instead as I haven't got any money. At least I get paid that way!

Sorry, forgot to introduce myself – I am Angela Fenwick, eighteen years old, boring brown hair that I've just had streaked, nice boobs and a good bum, and did I mention that I had finished with school? Yippee!

My Dad is a mad professor, who spends hours tinkering away at things that none of us understands, but it would appear that at last he seems to be at the end of his latest and longest mammoth project, which means either that he has got it working, or he has moved on to something else. Anyway, who cares, the good bit is that he and Mum are taking my best friend, Susan, my brother John – dead brainy, but he's all right - and me away for a short holiday. Susan was due to go off with her boyfriend, but she rang me last night to say that he had dumped her and she was miserable as sin, so I asked Mum and Dad if we could take her with us to cheer her up.

Susan was my best friend at school and has spent large amounts of time at our house, because her parents got divorced, which all means that she has become a virtual member of our family and hence is always known as my parents' *second daughter*. Mum and Dad said that of course she could come with us, which is great because she is going off to Exeter to do media studies and I won't see her for ages.

Rather than leaping over to Germany to see the outlaws, we are heading up to the Lake District to trace part of my Dad's family history. Sounds a bit boring, but the good news is that we get to visit the Bartons on the way, who used to live next to us and their son Jake is my bestest friend in the world – apart from Susan of course. I used to fancy him rotten when I was younger. Still do to be honest. We have kept in touch via email and now Facebook – isn't the Internet brilliant?

John and I call Jake's Mum and Dad Uncle Bill and Aunt Janet as they have always seemed like part of the family - Jake, John and I used to live in one another's houses all the time when we were growing up - and they live in a big posh house up in Cheshire. We're going to spend a couple of nights with them and then toddle off up to the Lake District. Cool.

*

'Are we nearly there yet?' we chorused from the back of the car like a group of five-year-olds.

'The SatNav says thirteen minutes, and I have no reason to think that Doris is lying,' Dad replied in a slightly resigned voice. We've only asked about five times, so I wasn't sure why he was upset just yet! I should also explain here that Dad calls the SatNav Doris, because it has a female voice – don't ask, just go with the flow. Fourteen minutes later (we got stuck behind a moron in a Skoda for a while) we were buzzed through the gates and up the drive to the Bartons' house. Jake's scrummy golden retriever called Mutt, after Muttley from the Dastardly and Muttley characters in Wacky Races, came bounding towards us and then Jake appeared at the front door hand-in-hand with some gorgeous looking girl – WHAT, I didn't remember seeing her on Facebook?

'Hi, welcome one and all, come through, Mum's just put the kettle on and Dad is coming in from the garden. Mutt, SIT! Hello John... hello Susan... and Angela, like the hair, come here and give me a hug.' Well, I didn't need asking twice, so I gave him a big cuddle and a friendly kiss, and then looked enquiringly at the leggy blonde (ouch, she was even better looking close up).

'Oh, sorry, this is my girlfriend Liz – we met at the tennis club a couple of weeks ago.'

Polite nods, followed by air kisses and we grabbed the bags and piled in. I couldn't wait to catch up on all of Jake's gossip. Jake showed us up to our rooms – the house was enormous, but then his Dad does something in hedge funds or whatever, and they have always been well off.

'Did you pack your bikinis as requested?' Jake grinned at Susan and me. We've been given a room to share with its own en-suite and everything - cool.

'Of course,' I replied, 'some of us are efficient!'

'OK – pool's in the back garden, last one in is a sissy!' he laughed and ran off with Liz to get changed – I bet she looks fabulous in a bikini – miaaooww, kindly pass me two saucers of milk.

Transpired the swimming pool was next to the tennis court – where else? We have beaten Jake and Liz down by a couple of minutes, and yes she did have legs up to her armpits, but I reckoned my cleavage was much better than hers. Let's not beat about the bush, Susan and I reckoned she looked like a stick insect with two fried eggs, if you really want to know! Anyway swimming pools are excellent places for lots of rowdy games and *accidental* grabs at other people, so there was plenty of opportunity for Jake to notice that I have *matured* considerably since he last saw me. Liz didn't swim, of course, as it would have disturbed her make-up and she took the opportunity to lie around like a beached lizard, and soak up some rays.

I couldn't quite get over the size of the house they have. When they lived next to us, their house was pretty large, but this had a snooker room, a family room, a den with all sorts of games consoles, a study/library (boring, for his Dad), a home cinema, and several others I have forgotten. Apparently it had belonged to some overpaid footballer who started putting most of his wealth up his nose, so Jake's Dad grabbed it at a good price. Whatever! It was magic, and we ran round the place like a bunch of excited school kids, which I suppose is exactly what we were until a short while ago.

Over dinner I decided that Liz was a total pain in the arse. Couldn't really see what Jake saw in her. All she talked about was how she spent one hundred pounds on a pair of designer jeans on Friday and *Have you seen the new handbags from blah-di-blah – they are simply to die for?* Yuck, pass me the sick bag rapidomente, she was worse than those bloody WAGs. John grinned at me across the table and mimed putting two fingers down his throat. She must be really foul if John noticed, he normally didn't get upset by anyone. Still, shut up and smile, Jake was still as gorgeous as ever and I was sure he wouldn't stay hooked up with this clothes-hanger for long, and we were coming back again next week on the way home – they had just invited us. Time enough to work the old Angela sultry magic I thought, and see what I could achieve.

'So what wondrous invention are you working on at present, Harold?' I heard Jake's Dad ask. He always pretended to wind my Dad up a bit about his inventions, but the truth was that he had funded a couple of Dad's projects in the early days and they have both made pots of money from them. As Dad kept reminding us, it had paid for our *expensive* education and lots of other goodies, so we shouldn't knock it. He was right there. John and I had both gone to the local village primary school, which was ace, but the secondary school down the road was the pits. Luckily that was when the money started to come in and Dad moved us to a different school, which was way better.

I could see John leaning forwards to hear what was being said, because Dad had been extremely cagey about his latest project and we knew nothing either.

'Bill, please don't be upset when I don't tell you about the latest project, but I think it would put you in an awkward position at work. I honestly think you could fall foul of insider trading regulations, but in a couple of weeks' time I promise I will reveal all.'

My Mum started to interrupt, 'Oh surely Harold you could tell Bill as your oldest friend?'

'I'm sorry, darling, but we have discussed this at length. This is simply one thing that has to stay quiet until the conference at the end of the month. I really am very sorry Bill, but I promise you will be the first to know the full details,' and he looked somewhat accusingly across the table at her.

Mm, interesting, obviously been some aggro going on there I thought. Mum and Dad didn't always see eye to eye, especially when it came to saving the planet, which was Dad's big hang-up. He wanted people to become far more eco-friendly and worry about leaving the planet in a fit state for their children and grandchildren. Mum went along with it all as long as it didn't interfere too much with her golf and social life.

Anyway, at that point the conversation dropped into Dad's favourite topics – namely everything that was wrong with the world, the incompetent politicians, *the dreadful rubbish they called TV comedy nowadays* (Dad's words), the dangerous greed of the banking system and a few others. Dad was renowned for his views and has been interviewed on TV many a time, because he *provided good value*. Well, that's what he claimed! He even suggested a new programme called *Eviction* to the company that makes some of the most popular shows. His idea was that the country should vote every week for the most unpopular people and they should be chucked out of the country at the end of the show. Virtually chucked out, not physically, but he reckoned they would get the idea, and he knew who would be the grand winner – *that two-faced lying git*. Then his least favourite person in the world retired and handed over to *an incompetent thieving git* and the TV Company thought there were too many shows like that already. Shame, could have been fun.

'What are we doing tomorrow?' I asked to break the somewhat boring discussion – well we had heard most if it all from Dad several times before. Liz looked totally uninterested by the question, which was pretty obvious as the shops wouldn't be open, but Jake answered by saying that he had planned a nice long walk for all of us along Alderley Edge, followed by a good pub lunch, which suited Mum and Dad down to the ground as they love hiking for miles. That sounded like several hours of Liz being pissed off, so that was good news to me too. She probably hadn't got a pair of shoes without 4-inch heels anyway!

After dinner I managed to grab Jake, without Liz, for a few minutes in the family room.

'How's Uni then?' I asked him as he had been at Leeds for a couple of years and I wanted to know what it was really like.

'Well Mutt misses me like mad, don't you, you stupid old thing?'

Mutt immediately rolled over on his back and went all soppy, and we both gave him a good old scratch and cuddle. He has the most wonderful eyes, which stop you in your tracks and make you forget about what you were thinking or doing. Mutt, I mean, although Jake is not far behind!

'Actually, apart from missing this old feller, it's magic,' Jake told me, 'but you have to take care not to lose track. It is very easy to get caught up in all of the social activities and forget about the work you're meant to be doing. The first year was quite easy, but this year has been a lot tougher. Next year's finals are going to be pretty gruesome I fear.'

'Yes, but you're a brain-box, so you'll be all right won't you?' I teased him.

'One of the things you learn really quickly at Uni is that there are an awful lot of people way cleverer than you studying there as well. We have one guy in our year, who is absolutely mind-blowing.' Jake stuck a great big grin on his face and winked at me. 'Fortunately he likes beer as well, so I can normally bribe him for a bit of help if I get stuck! You've been accepted at Canterbury haven't you? Pretty place and lots of nice pubs down there.'

At that moment Liz, the walking designer label, came back in from slapping a new layer of make-up on, so I reluctantly let her have Jake back again. He's way too good for you, I thought to myself. Sweet old Mutt agreed with me and walked away from her and over to me, which only proved what extremely good taste he has. So Mutt and I joined Susan and started discussing the "how-can-I-get-Jake-away-from-that-tedious-titless-tart" campaign.

Chapter 3

The Professor and Bill Barton were striding along ahead of the others as they walked along Alderley Edge. The air was wonderfully fresh, Mutt was ranging far and wide sniffing out rabbits, and the only sounds were the birds and an occasional child's laugh from another group of walkers. Up above there was scarcely a cloud in the sky and a couple of vapour trials crossed lazily miles above them.

'Bill, isn't this what it is all about?' the Professor said with a happy smile on his face.

Fortunately Bill knew his friend very well, and could guess where his mind was going most of the time. 'What do you mean Harold? Pretty scenery, the open air, a happy family, no mobile phones... all of the above?'

'Spot on, young William! That's exactly what I mean. We have a family that we dote on, children, who appear to love us, although you sometimes wonder if it's us or our wallets they love,' the Professor continued with a grin, 'and we can come out here and enjoy beautiful countryside. We can't let things like family values disappear and we can't let ignorant idiots ruin the planet.'

Bill was used to his friend going on about the planet, but he had the feeling there was a bit more to this than one of Harold's rants. 'You're worried about all of this, I can see, and knowing you, you have something up your sleeve?' he asked.

'Good try! Yes Bill, I have something up my sleeve, and I will tell you about it as soon as I can. It's probably the most important thing I have ever worked on and I am going to make sure that no governmental cretin cocks it up.' He looked at his friend and could see that Bill was chomping at the bit to know what his latest invention was, but Bill had known him for years and knew that when the Professor didn't want to talk about something, there was no point in asking.

'OK, I promise not to ask any more about that, so let's talk about the other stuff,' said Bill moving the conversation on to more fertile territory. 'Like you, I am deeply worried. I see the family unit breaking down. I see a generation of children – fortunately not ours – brought up on junk food and PlayStations, who as a result have no social skills and suffer from obesity. And I know that you see a planet that we don't really understand being raped by governments and corporations in their insatiable greed,' he paused for a second, 'but Harold, even you can't cure all that lot!'

'True, I'm not going to solve all the problems of the

world overnight. No-one can. And I'm extremely glad to see those TV chef chappies doing the programmes about crap food – did you see that one a while back where they cut open the dead body of an obese person?' Bill nodded that he had. 'I'm dreadfully squeamish as you know, and fall apart at the sight of a needle, but that had me riveted to the TV. Also made me change my diet because I hadn't realised how much hidden salt and sugar there was in some of the stuff I like. Gudrun has got us drinking less too. It's so easy to have your gin and tonic at 6 o'clock, and then have a bottle of wine with dinner every night.'

Bill looked crestfallen at this, as he had selected some extremely good Margaux to have with dinner that night. 'You haven't given up alcohol completely have you Harold? No, you were drinking the Chablis happily last night and I've got some very nice Chateau Lascombes for tonight!'

'No, Bill, we haven't given up. We have just cut down! A nice Margaux is definitely not to be ignored!'

The look of relief on Bill's face was huge. He didn't throw alcohol down his throat like the youth of today with their binge drinking, but he did enjoy a really good wine with his dinner.

'I must say you had me going there for a moment, because I thought we both followed the same scheme of bringing up our children the French way; namely having wine as part of the meal from an early age so that they learn to drink responsibly rather than it being a banned substance and making it appear far more attractive that way?'

The Professor nodded his agreement, 'Exactly. Just like that stupid Prohibition lark in America. Ban something and it goes underground and generates money and gangsters. I've always maintained that the Americans have an uncanny knack of taking something sensible and then regulating it so much that it a) drives everyone mad and b) loses all its initial purpose. Political correctness, for instance, which started as something sensible and has now almost ended up as a farce. If someone is a short, fat git, why on earth can't I call him or her that rather than having to say he/she is horizontally, vertically and intellectually challenged? Load of cobblers. And don't start me on their lunatic practice of suing one another for asinine reasons, a trait which unfortunately seems to be working its way across the pond.' The Professor had worked up a good head of steam, because he loved talking to Bill, who kindly let him rant on for a while and get things off his chest. They walked on for a while in silence and then Bill looked across at the Professor and picked up the conversation again.

'So what are you going to do about it all? I share your concerns about family and diet, and would dearly like all fast-food places to be shut down, and someone on TV recently sensibly suggested that cooking should be taught again at school,' said Bill, whose wife shared cooking as a hobby with Gudrun.

'Yes, and bring back some bloody sport as well. Stop all this crap about *they can't be allowed to lose, it's not good for them*. Total bollocks. They've got to learn that you don't win all the time. Unfortunately they all seem to be growing up with the impression that you don't have to work for anything, just sit on your arse, take out more credit and buy what you want.' The Professor paused for breath. 'Actually that is one thing I wanted to ask you. We are trying to work out how to fund Angela at University. I don't want her to starve, of course, but on the other hand I don't believe in handing our children everything on a plate. Do you mind my asking what you are doing with Jake?'

There followed a conversation on the allowance that Bill was giving Jake, from which he had to pay for everything. If he wanted something extra, then he worked for it, and was currently working in one of the local pubs to finance the car he had bought himself.

'It's not the most wonderful car in the world, but it is safe, and he loves it. Our neighbours assumed I would go out and buy him some smart new sports car, but like you I think that doesn't teach them the value of money and having to earn it themselves. It's amazing how designer labels suddenly don't seem nearly so important to Jake when he is the one paying for them!' Bill and Harold had had this conversation before, and had both been waiting for their children to come to their senses. 'He has also started playing a few gigs with some friends. Do you remember when he hated those piano lessons at school, and you started him off on the guitar as you thought it might give him some more *street cred*?' asked Bill, and the Professor nodded remembering a small child who was fascinated by music but bored to tears with playing the same old classical pieces. 'Well, I am not sure whether to thank you or not, Harold, because the noises coming out of our summerhouse when they practise are pretty awful, but they love it and I'd rather they were doing that than smoking dope and playing silly buggers. In fact, I think they are due for a practice session tonight, so you'll be able to hear if he's got any better!'

The Professor looked very happy as that fitted in with his ideas exactly. The last thing he wanted was for his daughter to come out of University saddled with some huge student debt, that would take her years to pay off, but on the other hand he wasn't going to let her lead a life of idle luxury whilst she was studying.

'OK, thanks for sharing that Bill. Interesting you should mention drugs – I'll come back to that later. As I told you, I've been thinking about that issue a lot,' he looked serious as he took up the conversation again at the point he had broken off. 'I know I'm being a bit harsh, and I have a lot of sympathy for the kids of today as lots of them appear to be almost wrapped in cotton-wool, and bored rigid. We did sport all the time, and then had youth clubs and things to go to in the evening – what do they have now? In fact, I have come to the conclusion that most of the fault lies with the parents rather than the kids – stick the little darlings in front of the TV / games console / PC or whatever and ignore them. I frankly can't make up my mind whether Bill Gates should be considered a hero or a complete villain, for ruining millions of peoples' lives.'

'Harold, I'm with you, and I've read your blog, so I know what gets you upset, but as I said before, what are you going to do about it all?' Bill asked.

'Yes, you're right,' sighed the Professor, 'I am going on a bit aren't I? Sorry about that, I think it's just the frustration of not being able to do anything that gets me.'

'That's why I like to come out here and clear my head when everything is going tits up,' said Bill. 'I find that you get a sense of perspective out here, and it cheers me up to see *a green and pleasant land*.' One again, the two of them looked around and smiled to see what they considered to be the best of things British.

'You're right Bill, I may despise the useless load of cretins running this country, but I wouldn't move. Well, I tried to persuade Gudrun to move to New Zealand, which to me is like the UK thirty years ago, but she quite rightly pointed out that we have family and friends over here and you can't just up roots and abandon them all. No, the countryside in the UK is magic, and on a day like this with no bloody idiots shouting down their mobile phones it really is heaven on earth.' He paused and took a long deep breath of fresh air. 'The lungs of the planet,... we must preserve the planet..... just look at Mutt enjoying himself ...now, where's that pub young Jake promised us, and tell me how he's getting on at Leeds – I've been boring you for far too long!'

'No more than usual!' his friend retorted with a wicked smile.

*

Bill and the Professor were sitting on the patio relaxing after a sumptuous dinner, when the strains of Jake's band wafted across from the summerhouse.

'Ah, if music be the food of love, play on,' murmured Bill. 'I suppose you want to go down and listen, don't you Harold?'

'You know me far too well. Do you mind?'

'Of course not. I'd actually like someone with a musical ear to let me know if they are rubbish or not.'

As they got closer to the summerhouse, Harold could hear that they certainly were not rubbish. The sounds coming out were definitely not those made by a bunch of people with no idea how to play their instruments. He knew from his own limited playing with other people that the sign of a band that was playing well was a tightness between the players, which only came from practice and a recognition of exactly who was going to play what and when. It was all too easy for each member to try and show off their skills all the time, which just led to people playing over one another – the combination and interplay of instruments was what the Professor liked, which was why he was currently going through all the Beatles songs at home studying the arrangements to see how they used the juxtaposition of instruments to achieve their amazing range of songs.

They quietly slipped in through one of the summerhouse doors and were not surprised to see Angela and Susan sitting on the ground with a couple of tambourines joining in. At the end of the song, Jake noticed they were there and looked enquiringly at Harold.

'What do you think, Uncle Harold, did your lessons pay off?'

'Excellent, and I'm not just saying that to please you! My only comment would be that I think it is a diminished in the last chorus, rather than the E minor 6th you were playing?'

The rest of the group looked amazed that some old bloke should even know the names of the chords let alone recognise what they had been playing, but as they tried the two different combinations they looked up in agreement.

'We played that song last time I did a gig with my friend's band and we made exactly the same mistake – you probably downloaded a chord sheet from the Internet?' Jake nodded. 'Thought so – you have to be careful with a lot of those as they are not always totally accurate.'

Jake smiled at Harold and pointed at a spare keyboard sitting unused. 'Want to join in?' Angela was amazed to find her Dad could actually hold his own with a bunch of young lads playing songs she thought he had never even heard.

As they walked back up to the house, Angela looked at her Dad and asked him where he had heard the songs before.

'Ah, to be honest, I only knew half of them; some because I've heard them or played them and one or two because they aren't actually new – I know the originals!' Angela and Susan rolled their eyes as the

Professor had frequently bored them to tears by extracting an old LP or CD from his extensive collection and playing them the original version of a song they thought they had just discovered.

'But how did you know what to play on the unknown ones – I didn't think you could play stuff by ear like your Grandad used to?'

'No, I am not nearly as good as my Grandad, who as you know could go up to London, listen to a show and then come home and play the whole thing without a note of music. No, I cheated a bit, and simply looked at Jake's fingers. As I play the guitar as well, it was easy for me to see what chords he was playing; combine that with a bit of musical knowledge and some improvisation, and hey presto you can join in with most pop tunes. That's how I learnt a lot of stuff when I was young – I just watched what chords they were playing on *Top of the Pops*. Where was Liz by the way?'

'Oh, she doesn't like loud music,' said Angela and Susan with a knowing look between them.

Chapter 4

The cottage was nestled in a little fold in the hills in an absolutely exquisite part of the Lake District. There were roses and clematis climbing up either side of the front door, and the garden was awash with a riot of colour. The herbaceous borders in the front garden were quintessentially English and the Professor wanted to dig them up and take them home with him.

The drive up had been relatively easy; the new toll-way round Birmingham made all the difference, avoiding the tedious choke point where the M5 and M6 meet. The stop-over with the Bartons had been a very pleasant break along the way, and they had been invited to spend the night again on the way back, so they could really relax and enjoy themselves.

They had come up here as the Professor wanted to research his family history and he had a picture of the family gravestone given to him years ago by his now dead Aunt. His mother had told him that his particular branch of the family was from Ireby, although the origins of the family actually traced back to the infamous cattle reivers on the borders of England and Scotland. That would be the next trip, they had decided. Do that one in peace and quiet when he had retired, without the children, but with some golf clubs. For the moment, the family plus their *second daughter* Susan were here to enjoy the views, celebrate the successful end of the Professor's project, their daughter's acceptance at Canterbury and their son's GCSEs. They also hoped they could cheer up Susan and throw in some geocaching along the way.

'So what exactly is this geocaching thing I've let myself in for?' asked Susan, with a sly glance at the Professor's son John, who had put her up to asking the question.

'Oh yes, I'd forgotten that we had never dragged you out on one of our caching trips before. Well,' began the Professor, 'you know all about GPS devices because you've used them in your field trips?' Susan nodded agreement. 'Geocaching is quite simple really. People have hidden caches – no money I am afraid, just little plastic boxes with a logbook and pencil in normally – and published their location on the Internet. Your task is to program the location into your GPS device and then go off and find them.'

'That all sounds very easy,' Susan replied, looking puzzled, 'where's the problem?'

'Ah, thought you might ask that,' grinned the Professor. 'Firstly, the devices are pretty accurate, but still you are probably looking for something that may only be the size of a 35mm film canister in a ten foot or more radius, and secondly we like doing the ones where people set puzzles you have to solve to get the coordinates in the first place.'

'Yes, a right pain he got to be with those puzzle ones!' interjected the Professor's wife, who was checking out the kitchen and finding that it was surprisingly well equipped, and it looked like she could actually indulge her cookery hobby whilst they were up here for a few days. 'He became totally obsessed with his bloody geocaching for a time – it was geocaching morning, noon and night, desperately trying to be the first to solve the puzzles, or setting ones that the other geocaching gurus couldn't solve straight away.'

'At least I didn't go out in the pitch dark looking for them like *Binary* and *Got2Bfirst*!'

The Professor could see that Susan was totally confused. 'We all use silly names for ourselves, to protect the innocent, although most of us know one another's real names now anyway! But, that's not important. There are some cachers, whose thing is to be the first to find – FTF in caching parlance – and they will go out in the middle of the night and the pouring rain to nab a cache before anyone else. Bloody mad, in our opinion! *Got2Bfirst* is the worst, think you can see where his name comes from now? And *Binary* - he works in computers - is not far behind. I was getting a bit like that .... '

'A bit?!' his wife threw in, with a grimace on her face.

The Professor smiled indulgently at her and continued. 'But actually meeting up with the gurus made me see how time-consuming the whole thing could become. Then we met up with some other cachers for a hunt one day, and discussed why we do the whole caching thing in the first place. Well, that's when we realised that the real reason for doing it was to go for nice walks in beautiful countryside and enjoy the views. Look, it's much easier if I just show you the website – come with me and I'll fire up the laptop.'

When booking the cottage the Professor had checked that they had a broadband connection, as he couldn't face the slow painful slog of dial-up, so a short while later they were huddled round the Professor's laptop having a look at all the caches round where the cottage was located. Susan could not believe how many of them there were, and the Professor explained that last time he had looked there were over half a million active caches round the world, and there were hundreds of cachers in the UK alone. There were even some caches in Antarctica, he told her, although for obvious reasons they weren't visited too often. She was amazed as she had assumed it was basically a small bunch of saddos, wearing anoraks, but they appeared to be normal people much to her surprise.

The Professor explained the basic rules. A cache always contained a log book, so that you could record your find, which you also entered on the relevant cache page on the geocaching website. That way everyone could see which caches had been found and you could notify the owner if there were any problems.

'To confuse you even further,' said the Professor with a wry grin, 'we have our own language. Non-cachers are called Muggles, as in Harry Potter, and if you get stuck you can always PAF – Phone A Friend. When people find a cache they often write TFTC – Thanks for the Cache, and TNLN – Took Nothing Left Nothing.'

'What can you take?' asked Susan, looking totally bemused. 'I thought you said there was only a logbook and pen?'

'Sorry, I didn't explain properly. There's always a logbook and a pen or pencil if there's room. The bigger the cache – they go from the size of a finger-tip to big boxes – the more they have in them. The bigger caches typically have a few cheap plastic toys or similar for the children. Some have those cheap cameras in them so you can take a photo. The rules are that you can take something out if you replace it. The idea is that kids get to do a treasure hunt and hence enjoy going on walks with their parents, rather than moping around the house playing computer games!'

The Professor was very keen on the idea that kids should get out and do some exercise rather than sitting indoors. He worried about the Internet generation growing up, who could only spell in SMS-text language, had limited social interaction, and were mainly obese. In fact, one of his jokes was that Darwinism would create a generation of children with no legs, two thumbs and limited brain power – the punch line was that in his opinion it already had!

'Last, but not least, for the moment, there are also

things called Travel Bugs.'

'Travel Bugs? Sounds nasty,' was Susan's comment as she wrinkled her nose in mock horror.

'Nothing dangerous,' the Professor assured her. 'You simply buy a little dog tag, attach it to the item of your choice, and then you send it off round the world with a mission. We have one called *Grumpy Old Men*, whose mission is simply to cheer people up. I've taken ones over to America, picked ones up in Spain, South Africa – they are all over the place. It's all slightly nerdy, but you can actually see in Google Earth where they have been on their travels, which is quite sweet, and you get a message every time it moves on. Last time I looked, *Grumpy* was in Manchester.'

Susan was beginning to think she had entered a parallel universe, but Angela grinned at her and told her not to worry. 'The first time we went out with Dad we thought he was bonkers! But then Dad found the first cache and we saw just how accurate these GPS things are now. Then it was a fight to see who could find the next one!'

'Yes, I remember that,' said the Professor with a big smile, 'and we all ended up at a very convenient pub on Epsom Downs – perfect.'

'Only because I allowed you to open your Christmas present early!' interjected his wife with a cheeky grin.

'True, but you must agree it is probably the most used and useful present you have ever bought me?' replied the Professor.

'So where are we going tomorrow?' Susan asked.

'Well,' grinned the Professor with a twinkle in his

eye, 'there are not many puzzle caches round here, as most people are setting up caches to simply encourage people to do the famous Lake District walks.' He fired up another window, went into Wikipedia and looked up Wainwright. He then showed them all the information about the famous hill walker, guidebook author and illustrator Alfred Wainwright, whose seven-volume *Pictorial Guide to the Lakeland Fells* had become the standard reference work to the two hundred and fourteen fells of the Lake District.

'Don't worry,' he cried as they all looked concerned by the number, 'we are only doing a couple. Tomorrow we are going to do a nice easy family walk called Catbells: to quote Wainwright *"It is one of the great favourites, a family fell where grandmothers and infants can climb the heights together, a place beloved. Its popularity is well deserved, its shapely topknott attracts the eye offering a steep but obviously simple scramble."* That will do nicely for tomorrow and then there are a couple of caches near here that I can't resist for later in the week – *Cockup View* and *Heffalump's Peak* – they sound perfect for us! Now, let's all help your mother get the dinner ready and lay the table.'

One of the things that Gudrun had introduced at home was a nice big round kitchen table so that the whole family, including their *second daughter*, could sit together at meal time. They had a dining room, but didn't use that every day and Gudrun wanted to ensure that they all got together at least once a day so that they could talk to one another. She and the Professor had seen too many families, where the children were off doing their own thing, and they didn't like it. The families in some other countries seemed to be a lot closer than in the UK and they thought a lot could be learnt from that.

The Internet and computers might be wonderful things, but to them family life was more important. Tonight was a classic example where Susan and Angela wanted to talk about University and all the implications thereof, which gave the Professor the chance to tell them what he had learnt from Bill about Jake's life, accommodation and financial arrangements at Leeds.

'So where is this Catbells thing?' asked John when the University conversation had died down.

'It's the other side of Keswick,' explained his father, 'so we will drive down there tomorrow. The easiest option then is to take a trip on the *Derwentwater Motor Launch*, which will take us across the lake to the starting point for the walk up the Fell. Right, let's clear this lot up and have an early night as I am going to march you across the fells tomorrow!'

The children pretended to be horrified by the prospect, but they knew their Dad was just teasing, and there was bound to be a nice pub and a decent lunch somewhere en route. Their parents loved to walk their legs off, but they always made sure there was sustenance provided along the way.

Chapter 5

The Professor had been wanting to come to the Lake District for years. It never ceased to amaze him how much beautiful landscape there was on your doorstep in the UK, which people chose to ignore in their desperate hunt for sunshine and cheap alcohol.

He and his wife had a simple system on holiday; if the people coming the other way spoke English, then they started talking German to one another. If the people were speaking German, then they spoke English. The funniest trip had been on a flight down to Australia for a Conference, where the Professor had used some of his Air Miles to take his wife along with him. They were sitting on the top deck of a jumbo, when a very loud German couple came in behind them with the husband complaining loudly in rude German about the lack of space for his bag and his video camera. His wife had begged him to be quiet as someone might understand German, but he had ignored her.

An hour or so later the cabin attendant came past asking what everyone wanted for dinner, but couldn't remember the German for smoked salmon, so the Professor and his wife helpfully explained what it was called in German, and Gudrun smiled sweetly and said that as she was German she was happy to help with any other words. The look from behind had been absolutely classic, and not another word was heard from the couple the whole trip until the purser came up to the Professor and his wife and asked if they would like to sit in the cockpit for the landing at Brisbane, at which point the German husband nearly had a heart attack! The Professor grinned as he reminded his wife of that trip.

The areas they had driven through so far were picturesque and he was really looking forwards to exploring some of the quieter and more remote parts. Keswick was a bit too busy for his liking, but it gave him a great excuse to take them all out on the water and start them off with a pleasant and hopefully not too strenuous hike. He had seen a programme on the television about the Catbells walk, and it hadn't looked too tricky. He had done some research on the web, and had got some estimates of timings and distances; he had also found another site with recommendations of what they should carry with them. This wasn't like going for a stroll in the Surrey countryside; the weather up in the hills and mountains could change very quickly so they had maps, the GPS and a compass, waterproof jackets, some food, and a basic first aid kit in case of blisters or whatever.

The Keswick Launch was a pretty little boat. The Professor's father had been mad keen on boats and he would have loved the trip round the lake. Unfortunately he died of cancer when the children were very young, which was a shame as he had a wicked sense of humour and would have loved to lead his grandchildren astray. The Professor's research told him that they had plenty of time, and as the weather was so nice they took the long route round the lake stopping at Ashness Gate, Lodore, High Brandelhow, and Low Brandelhow before finally disembarking at Hawse End for the start of the climb.

'Catbells is only 1481 ft high, but it rises quite rapidly. So the views should open up quickly, which is probably one of the reasons why it is one of the popular walks,' he read from a guide book as they made their way up the zigzag path. Judging by the number of people out and about, it was definitely popular, and the views were getting better all the time. In one direction you could see across Derwentwater to Saddleback, while in the other direction there were fine views across to Skiddaw.

'Who is Thomas Arthur Leonard?' asked Angela as she spotted a memorial plaque on one of the rocky outcrops.

'Ah, I knew you would spot that plaque, so I looked him up,' said the Professor, looking for a piece of paper in his rucksack. 'Here we are, you'll wish you'd never asked! The Rev Thomas Arthur Leonard, a Congregational Minister, was born in Stoke

Newington in 1864. A group from his Young Men's Guild took a holiday at Ambleside in 1891 and at Caernarvon in 1892. By 1893 Leonard became honorary secretary of a scheme for summer rambling holidays with social evenings of music and lectures. What I believe you young folks call binge drinking nowadays?' he enquired with a cheeky grin.

They discovered that there are two parts to the walk. The path had reached a minor summit and they stopped for refreshments and to admire the views. The path then led on along a level ridge for while, which lulled them into a false sense of security, because they discovered that the final ascent to the true summit was pretty steep and there were several rocky bits. However, they weren't as daunting as they appeared and they were soon on the summit.

The views were spectacular, and they stood there for a while soaking it all in. The Professor got his camera out and starting taking a series of photos to stitch together into a panorama. He had his new lens with him – a real kick-arse job as his daughter so sweetly put it when she first saw it. He would have described it slightly differently. It was actually a wide-angle zoom with a nice big aperture and Image Stabilisation, which meant he could take some seriously good photos.

He would have liked to bring the rest of his camera kit with him, but he had long ago realised that serious photography takes time and patience and he could not expect the rest of them to stand around bored rigid for hours whilst he set up his tripod and waited for the correct lighting. Anyway, his best photos were taken very early in the morning or late in the evening, when the lighting was much more interesting, and the shadows tended to show a lot more texture in the landscape.

In fact, they discovered that when you stand at the summit of Catbells the panorama is exceptional in both senses; there are some simply great views and also some good contrasts. The Professor took his son to one side and they studied the landscape, as John was studying geography at school and the Professor thought he would be intrigued by the differences around them.

'The hills to the north are smooth in outline, Dad, whilst those to the south are rugged – do you see what I mean?'

His father nodded, 'And why's that do you think, my *favourite son*?'

John had heard the name so often that he didn't rise any more to stating that he was the only son, so he pondered for a moment and then said, 'I'm guessing the hills to the north are composed of slate, because we've seen a lot of that as we've been driving through?' His father nodded encouragement. 'Well, that erodes easily, which will make them smooth, but the hills to the south must be made of something else as they are resisting erosion?' The Professor showed his son the extract he had printed off, which confirmed the hills were actually of volcanic origin.

As they looked round they could also see the U-shaped valley of Borrowdale to the east, which was formed when a glacier once passed by, grinding away the sides of the fells. It reminded him of a brilliant trip they had made some years ago to Yosemite in the US. That was probably the first time that they had walked the children's legs off. They had hired one of the huge American camper wagons, or RVs as the Americans called them, and had driven to the Grand Canyon, Bryce Canyon, Zion Canyon, across through Yosemite to San Francisco and then down the fabulous coast road to Los Angeles to visit some friends, who were living out there. Yosemite was one of the Professor's favourite places he had been to, along with New Zealand. He loved raw nature and was very surprised by Yosemite. The Americans, in his humble opinion, were extremely good at ruining anything pretty by putting a string of fast-food restaurants through the middle of it, but the view as you drove through the tunnel and into Yosemite was simply one of the best views in the world, and the Americans had made sure it never got spoilt. They had camped under the trees in the middle of the park and the kids had loved it.

'The lakes you can see - Derwentwater and Bassenthwaite Lake - were once joined. Sediments then washed down in the rivers and streams and as you can see they have formed a plain between them. John can probably tell us all about that from his geography studies,' the Professor continued reading from his notes and looked across at his son.

John nodded his agreement. 'It's so different when you see it in real life.' he said. 'At school, it's a bit dry and technical. Here you can almost feel it happening. Bit like when we went to Yosemite,' and the whole family smiled as they thought back to that beautiful place.

'I know I am a Boring Old Fart,' started the Professor, one of whose nicknames in the family was Bof the Prof, 'but you have to admit this is magic. Gorgeous views, no mobile phones, and a pub on the way back! Do you remember that walk we did down by Frensham ponds, darling?'

The Professor and his wife had seen a walk published in the little *Surrey Matters* magazine that came through the letterbox. It went from Frensham Great Pond, through the village of Tilford with a lovely little pub on the cricket green, and then back via the Little Pond to the starting point. There were, of course, a couple of caches along the way. The kids started to look bored as their parents started remembering the caches and the walk.

'Hang on a moment,' said their Mum, 'John, you will be very surprised by who used to drink at the pub in the middle of the walk.'

'Oh yes, I'd forgotten about that – a very famous world Champion who died at the age of twenty-nine driving his car along the Guildford bypass from memory,' said the Professor.

John immediately leapt in with the correct answer of Mike Hawthorn, because he was a total nut on Formula 1, and started to tell them all about him. 'He won the 1958 championship from memory, with just one point more than Stirling Moss. He was driving for Ferrari, and then he got fed up with the whole thing, I think because his team mate got killed or something like that, and retired. That was just before he killed himself in that accident. Remember the Goodwood Festival of Speed was called *From Hawthorn to Hamilton* last year.'

'Yes indeed, well remembered, John. In that case you won't be at all surprised to learn that there is a cache dedicated to him, where you have to go and find his grave and the house where he lived and a couple of other things – would you like to do that one someday?' the Professor asked and John was sold.

'OK, that's a deal. We'll do that when we get back home. Now, sorry to bore you all...again, but I thought you should learn something about the area as well,' started the Professor. 'Anybody care to guess what those scars on the hillside are all about?'

He then went on to explain that this used to be a major mining area, with lead and copper being extracted back in the 1500s.

'The reason for mentioning it is, in fact, not to bore you, but because the miners who were brought in to exploit the minerals were actually German.' A fact that made his wife beam with pleasure. 'The German miners lived in isolation on that little island down there called Derwent Isle, but they must have found a way off now and then because some of them married local girls.' The children grinned as they thought of the miners trying to get a bit of nooky.

'From memory, the TV programme I saw said that in the 1900s fifty percent of the population up here was in mining. It was a big operation too, they hauled something like fifty to seventy thousand tons of lead out of here in the 1800s. They also got silver out and that went to the mint to make coins. What the TV programme said was that they needed money for armaments, so they brought the Germans over to get copper out of the ground. The copper got put in the coins to save money and that paid for the weapons. Sneaky. Anyway, just to worry you, somewhere under here they said there is a thousand foot hole from one of the mines, so don't go wandering off – all right?... It's ok, you're safe, they've blocked up all the openings, but the hole is under here somewhere. SPOOKY! Right down we go and much to your surprise you will find I have also checked where the pub is and programmed its location into my trusty GPS. *"The nearby Swinside Inn serves welcome refreshments all year round"* it tells me. Lead on McDuff.'

The weather had been kind to them, so the walk had been a pleasure. After a very pleasant lunch in the pub they made their way back to the car and drove back to Ireby to look for the family gravestone. They had a picture from the Professor's aunt and as they drove past the church at the end of the village the kids called out that they had spotted it. The Professor turned the car round and parked up by the church and there it was.

Generations of his family were recorded on the gravestone, and at the bottom a memorial to his uncle, who had tragically been killed at the end of the war in Sumatra. The sick part was that the war was actually over, but the enemy hadn't known that and his uncle had been killed as they were being evacuated. A stupid mistake and a stupid waste. The Professor had been named after his uncle, and to be standing here with all the spirits of his ancestors was a weird but somehow deeply satisfying feeling.

Chapter 6

'There is one more thing I need to tell you all before you settle down in front of the laptop,' stated the Professor in his serious voice. They were back in the cottage and were searching out the details of the caches for the next day's walk. Ah, they thought, this must be what he didn't want to talk to Bill Barton about the other night. The Professor had been super secretive on his latest project, so perhaps this was the moment of truth?

Hence he rapidly had their undivided attention, and continued. 'Apart from the obvious celebrations of Angela and Susan getting their places at University and John rattling off a most splendid collection of GCSEs, we have also come here to celebrate the successful culmination of my research work on the project that I have been working on,' and now they were all straining forwards like eager pets waiting for a treat.

'For years people have been trying to come up with an alternative to fossil fuels. Now, when I first started looking at all this, I must admit I was driven primarily by the green issues, trying to find something that wouldn't pump toxic gases into the atmosphere. The more I researched our dependence on fossil fuels and the alternatives though, the more I discovered some very alarming facts.' He paused for a second. 'A phrase you will hear more and more in the future is Peak Oil, which is the point where the rate at which we use oil exceeds the rate at which we discover new deposits. People are arguing over when this will be – not about whether it will happen, but when, and the worrying part is that we are talking very soon.'

'But, they are working on alternatives aren't they Dad, like solar and wind and nuclear and stuff?'

'Yes, but so far they have found nothing that will replace our dependence on fossil fuels quickly enough. Each of them, unfortunately, has pros and cons. For instance, solar panels are looking good in static locations, but not for cars; wind farms are not the most attractive thing in the world and again do nothing for transport; nuclear has all the ramifications of what to do with the waste, and you need large amounts of energy to extract the nuclear ore and process it; nuclear fusion is probably the solution if we can make it work, but no-one knows when that will be; biofuels seem to do more harm than good.' He checked they were following along. 'I could go on, but believe me that we aren't there yet, and what people forget is that we don't just use fossil fuels to generate electricity and drive our cars. Without fossil fuels, we have no food, no water distribution, no modern medicine, no banking system, no Internet – shall I carry on?' They all looked deeply shocked as the Professor revealed what was happening to the planet. 'As you can guess, this is what has got me really worried. If we don't solve the problem of a replacement for fossil fuels, life on this planet will change dramatically – I won't bore you further at this point, but I think you can think of the implications. The world as we know it would no longer exist – famine and strife would be rampant. In fact, I've got a novel here I have just read, which I recommend – it explores a world where the oil has been cut off, and it makes very frightening reading.'

They all looked at him as if he were slightly mad and Angela accused him of exaggerating, to which he replied that he wished he wasn't, and showed them a couple of websites that examined the whole issue. Having got their 100% attention he now told them he was going to use the world of the motor car as the one they knew best to explain what he had been up to.

'We have seen people go down the diesel route, but frankly diesels are not good in urban situations – the filters all clag up – and they are noisy and smelly, and don't solve the root problem.' He paused for a second to check they were all still following along. 'There is a lot of work on electric cars at present, but they are full of batteries that weigh a ton and you have to charge them up all the time. Then we have the hybrid jobs, which are a step in the right direction, but frankly aren't there yet. So the one I have been working on is the so-called fuel cell – a bit like a battery, but a battery is sealed and has to be recharged, which costs energy and hence pollution. In a fuel cell you supply fuel, for instance hydrogen, and an oxidant, for instance oxygen, and the cell will then operate virtually continuously.'

'Hang on, Dad, they had that on Top Gear recently,' John interrupted. 'The Japanese have just brought out a car with a fuel cell – the Honda Clarity from memory – James May went over to California to try it out and was saying it really was the car of the future. Oh yes, and he went to Jay Leno's amazing garage of cars and chatted to him – I looked up his garage on the Internet, it's got some fabulous stuff in it, a McLaren F1, an SLR McLaren, Porsches, Lambos etcetera etcetera - amazing.'

'Yes, I remember the programme. As it happens, I have been talking off and on with the Honda team for the last couple of years. By the way Jay Leno's mother comes from Scotland, so that's obviously why he's such a good chap!' The Professor watched all their mouths drop as he casually brought forth those nuggets. 'Now, if you remember what James said, the fundamental way that the car works is for the fuel cell to supply the power for an electric motor. So you get an electric car without a ton of batteries, and the only pollution is H plus O – water.'

'So, the whole thing's solved now isn't it?' asked John.

'Yes and no. As a bit of background, anyone like to hazard a guess as to where and when the fuel cell was invented?'

The general consensus was that they all thought it was something very recent, so they were amazed when the Professor told them it had been invented by a Welshman called William Robert Grove back in 1842.

'The good news is that the fuel cell is a lot more efficient than the internal combustion engine. They've obviously been working on them for a long time now, and they are getting better and better. In fact, you only need a few kg of fuel to keep a cell going for ages. Another little bit of trivia for you; what broke on Apollo 13 was the oxygen supply to the guess what – the fuel cells.' He paused to collect his thoughts. 'The big problem in fact is the fuel itself – the hydrogen.'

'What, extracting it?'

'That's part of it and I have been working with a couple of groups on methods for extracting it without creating any greenhouse gases, and we're getting there. The big problem is storing it, which you either have to do at extremely low temperatures to keep it liquid, or at very high pressures.' He stopped for a moment, before the big finale. 'And that is what I now have a working solution for.'

The Professor then went on to explain that as is the way with many breakthroughs he had to admit there had been a large degree of luck involved as he had been testing something else and happened upon it all by chance.

'Which also means that it is extremely unlikely that anyone else will stumble upon my *secret combination*,' he paused for dramatic effect, 'and what that all basically means is that cars won't need petrol or diesel any more, and the cost of motoring will go down dramatically, unless of course the Government in their infinite ignorance slap a sodding great tax on it ...'

'Harold – language!'

'Sorry, my love, but you know how much I detest politicians – waste of space most of them. Anyway, where was I? Oh yes, the cost will go down dramatically, and for me the thing that really matters is that it solves the Peak Oil problem and the pollution is nil. So no more ruining our planet by pumping tons of noxious gases into the atmosphere, and no outbreak of war as people fight over the last oil deposits.' The children looked stunned, but his wife looked angry.

'Yes, and you want to give it away, you stupid man,' she muttered.

'Yes, I do want to *give it away*. I believe the planet desperately needs our help, and my technology should be made available to all nations without having to go through tedious regulations and patents and God knows what else! Also, if one nation owns the technology and doesn't share it, it will lead to a complete shift of *political* power and God knows what other ramifications. The sad fact is that the nations who need cheap *electrical* power most are those that can least afford it.'

'There are other schemes out there,' he continued with slightly clenched teeth, 'but biofuels seem to cause more pollution than they actually save, and have caused world food prices to go through the roof. There's one idea based on processing rubbish, discarded plastic, old tyres etc. to make ethanol fuel. They reckon that will cost about fifty pence a gallon, but that still pollutes, and my fuel cell costs a fraction of that to run. Last but by no means least, with the current financial crisis in the world, we all desperately need something to kick start the economy and this just might be it.'

This was obviously an argument the Professor and his wife had had many times before, and neither was prepared to budge. The Professor had dreams of an eco-planet, which was not dependent on oil, and his wife appeared to have dreams of a villa on Barbados. John, Angela and Susan were of a generation, which was far more attuned to the perils of the planet and what the future would hold, so anything that cut down pollution got a thumbs-up in their book. Also the whole background about how dependent everything they took for granted was on fossil fuels had rather shattered their protected little world.

'Anyway, let's not argue now. I'm going to present my findings at the world Eco-Conference in London at the end of this month, which is why we can't stay up here longer than a week I am afraid. But, in the meantime, John and Angela, I need a quiet word with you both please.'

'I need John to pick me some beans from the garden for dinner, talk to Angela for the moment,' his wife commanded, who was obviously still in a huff from earlier, and wanted to get her own back. John looked well cheesed off, but the Professor smiled at him, and told him he would talk to him later on, so not to worry.

So the Professor took his daughter to one side and told her quietly that she needed to know something important, and he paused to make sure she was listening closely. He needn't have worried; she had always been the curious one in the family.

'OK, I obviously have all the details of all of this here on my laptop, and I have sent the prototype and a copy of my papers to my lawyers. But, I thought I would set up a challenge for you and your brother when we get back home. I have hidden a USB stick with all the important details in a cache down near where we live ... let me finish .... and no-one will find it as I've cheated a bit. I want you and John to find it when we get back home as a game to keep you occupied. If it all works, we'll hide something else in the final cache and publish them as a new series.'

Angela fortunately knew quite a lot about caching as she and her brother had often been used as guinea pigs for her Dad's latest caches, so he was making sense.

'You've done some of my caches before, so you know the basic principle, but I have had to be a bit inventive here as I want to set a challenge that you and John can crack, but I've had to set it all up so that no-one else can solve it, and yet still remain within the rules of geocaching.'

Angela looked slightly confused, but she could see where her father was coming from.

'As you know, when a cache is published normally, the information to find it should all be on the cache page, either as simple coordinates *North blah-di-*

blah/West blah-di-blah, or as a puzzle to solve.' Angela nodded, fine so far.

'You also have to enter the final location of the cache on the website. On a normal cache, everyone can see that, but on a puzzle cache, it is hidden from everybody, except the person hiding the cache – me - and the man who checks all the caches round where we live, and he is a volunteer who calls himself *Celo*.' Angela nodded again.

'So if I published the correct final location, it would be recorded on the website and *Celo* would be able to see it. Well my concern with that is someone might be able to hack in to look at it, or some nefarious character could persuade *Celo* to reveal all, so I couldn't really put the correct location on the website.'

Angela looked somewhat worried and confused by all of this, but he could see she was already working out the ramifications of a puzzle without a correct solution. Her Dad explained that when you publish a cache, all the details get checked by *Celo*, to ensure it was not on private land, not too close to other ones etc.

However, he had also checked with *Celo* what would happen if the police demanded he reveal the location of a puzzle cache. *Celo*, quite rightly, had explained that he would be duty bound to reveal the location. The Professor also explained that in today's world of hacking, he was convinced that someone would find a way of getting into the geocaching website and looking up the location.

'So,' her father explained, 'I couldn't go that route. If some unscrupulous person got wind of me hiding the

USB stick, they might try and get the location from *Celo*, or hack into the database. The only people I truly trust are you and your brother, as you have both always supported my love of the planet and I trust you to follow that path as you grow older?' Angela nodded.

'Your mother, God bless her, hates puzzles and would probably try to sell my work to the highest bidder. So let's go to Plan B.'

Plan B, he explained, entailed publishing the cache with a puzzle leading to the final location, but the final location in the cache listing, and hence the one *Celo* would have to reveal, was wrong. Yes, it was a bit sneaky, but at least it would keep the location safe. Also, he explained, whenever he set up a cache he put a link on the cache page to a special website called geochecker – this meant that anyone who had solved the puzzle could check their answer.

'They will get *Success* on geochecker, but that just means they have successfully found the wrong location. There is no way anyone can find the real location from the information on the webpage, or by asking *Celo*, or by hacking into the website, or from geochecker.'

There was a huge grin on the Professor's face. He loved logic problems, and to him this was an example of a slightly convoluted, but really rather elegant logic problem – how to publish, and at the same time, how not to give it all away. And last but not least, he explained that he had added a couple of extra measures to throw searchers off the scent.

'Just a minute,' his daughter's mental cogs were

whirring at top speed, 'what if they logged in as you and looked at your listings. Ah, no, that won't work will it as they will still see the wrong answer?'

'Excellent, my little piranha fish. I realised that you, or some *fiendish International criminal*, would probably cheat and try to login as me and simply look up the answer, so I am afraid that the answer on there is wrong anyway – ha, foiled, you cursed young whipper-snapper!'

The Professor had a huge grin on his face, because he loved setting and solving logic puzzles, something that he had inherited from his maths teacher at school, who always set an extra logic puzzle or two in the end of term exam. He had thought long and hard about how to manipulate the usual geocaching rules to get to the result he wanted, and as far as he could tell he had achieved his objective. But, as he was never satisfied with the simple approach, and always wanted to make sure he had a complete puzzle, he had added another couple of twists.

'Most cachers use their hobbies as a basis for their puzzles,' he continued, 'and the gurus know mine, so I have published this cache under a fictitious name. I have also listed some hobbies, which are so far removed from mine, that no-one will get anywhere near solving the cache from those! And, of course, I've thrown in a few red herrings in the attributes and the hints sections.'

There was silence for a couple of minutes as she worked through what she had just been told and then the questions came thick and fast.

'How long have you been working on all of this Dad?'

'Ah, I must admit it has taken a few months and quite a few emails back and forth to *Celo* to check what was allowed and what not,' her father replied with a twinkle in his eye.

'OK, so what is the fictitious name?' Angela asked.

'One that is obvious to you and your brother, and the email account associated with it has the same name at hotmail.co.uk,' her father said looking to see what she would ask next.

'What about the password?' was Angela's next question.

'Ah, good one! You know my standard system, and I've used that for the fictitious hotmail account. I've also sent an email to the hotmail account to give you a few hints.'

'How do we solve the puzzle if the obvious answer is wrong?' Angela asked next.

'And there,' grinned her father in appreciation of the question that really mattered, 'lies the rub. The hints on the geocaching website will purposely be meaningless and misleading to other people, but should be meaningful to you and your brother. I must admit, that's the bit I'm proudest of, even if I say so myself!' her father finished with an attempt at humility.

Angela reached for a pen and paper, and was heading towards the PC.

'Write nothing down, Gruntfuttock,' cried her father using a nickname he had called her for years, and which came from the Radio series *Round the Horne*. J

Peasemold Gruntfuttock was one of the characters in the series played by Kenneth Williams, and the name had always appealed to the Professor. 'You have all the information you need, even if you think I haven't given you enough. If in doubt, my final recommendation is to *think diagonally*. Now,' he announced in a much louder voice, so that everyone could hear, 'let's have a drink to celebrate – not just my work on the fuel cell, but much more importantly, all your exam results as well,' and he marched off towards the kitchen to get a bottle of champagne.

'Damn, I've not got enough cream,' her mother called from the kitchen, 'can one of you nip down to the little shop we passed on the way in and get a pint of single cream?'

John had already been out picking the beans, which meant he wasn't inclined to move again, so Angela told Susan to stay in the warmth (she was still trawling through the geocaching website and Google Earth). She grabbed her wind-jacket, popped on her hiking boots, hat and scarf as they were all ready by the door for tomorrow's outing, and set off.

Little did she know that her family and best friend were about to enter a world of terror.

Chapter 7

'Are you absolutely sure that you got everything from the house?' asked the Sheikh.

'As far as can be reasonably expected, without tearing down the whole house. Why, is there nothing on the PCs or in the safe?'

'Douglas and his colleagues have been working all through the night and all of today and found absolutely nothing. The Professor must have taken it with him – find out where he's gone and get it. Then make sure there are no loose ends.'

Those were the sort of orders Brutus liked. The Sheikh may have meant to make sure they had all the copies, but Brutus liked to *really tidy up* loose ends. Brutus put down the phone and called his team over.

'Here's the Professor's wife's mobile phone number – find them.'

A few minutes later Hojo had the answer, the Northern part of the Lake District.

'Get your weapons, just handguns will be enough, and bring the Range Rover round. We're going hunting.' Magic, life had been too quiet recently for his liking. He wondered if the Professor would put up a fight or just roll over. Probably the latter. Shame, he liked a bit of resistance, as it brought out the finer points of his interrogation technique, and the Professor deserved a good *talking to* as he had disturbed Brutus's carefully laid out plan.

Intercept the package going to the lawyer – done.

Clean out the house and collect any other copies – apparently incomplete.

Leave surprise for Professor inside his piano – done.

Let Professor blow himself to bits and hence stop him working on a replacement – potentially thwarted.

Well, he would just have to come up with an alternative when they found the Professor.

On the way up the motorway, they stopped to fill up with petrol and get some snacks. The guy in front of Brutus at the checkout was a complete imbecile. He got to the checkout, started putting all his purchases in a bag and then after an age eventually got round to pulling his wallet out to pay for everything.

'Hey, shitface,' said Brutus towering over the spotty-faced youth, 'did you pack your brain in their with your candy bars. Get your fucking money out ready you fuckwit and stop wasting my time!'

The young lad was about to argue, and then he looked at the size of Brutus and decided beating a hasty retreat was a much more sensible option. The garage attendant looked somewhat shocked by the whole thing, but he too decided that keeping quiet was the sensible option. Anyway, it was all captured on CCTV if the young lad wanted to make a complaint later.

Brutus paid the bill in cash and swaggered back to the car. He always felt good when he had put someone in their correct place. The useless fuckwit British youth all wandered round with their jeans hanging half way down their ass, thinking they looked cool. He certainly didn't want to know what underwear the little fuckwits were wearing and he was sure the assholes didn't know where the fashion of wearing pants that way started. That was a US penitentiary thing, where they took your belt away. Wearing your pants like that meant you had done time and you were hard. That little fuckwit was soft as marshmallow, he wouldn't have lasted thirty seconds in a US pen.

Fuck him.

He was lowlife.

Way below him.

And badly dressed.

Hardly worth the effort, but he still swaggered back to the car.

Chapter 8

I strolled down to the local shop, found the cream and checked out the magazines. Mum and I loved the trashy celebrity ones, and Dad of course despised them as he could see no point in reading about overpaid plonkers, who should be ignored. He didn't believe us when we told him that reading celebrity shite was actually a sign of high IQ! I chatted to the young girl serving there – holiday job, going to Durham to study history - and was just setting out for the cottage again when I nearly got knocked back into the shop by a black Range Rover driving far too fast through the village.

'Wankers,' I shouted after them, and gave them the finger. Lucky Mum and Dad weren't around or they would have given me a right bollocking. I grinned as I thought about Dad using the occasional fruity expletive when he didn't think Mum was listening. They weren't bad parents really, compared with what

I'd heard from my friends. Several had parents, who had gone through very acrimonious divorces, a couple of boys were definitely into drugs and one girl was either putting on weight very fast or was pregnant, which was hardly surprising as she was the school bicycle. Granny was convinced that sort of thing didn't happen at *nice schools in Surrey*. If she only knew!

As I turned the corner I saw the Range Rover going up the drive to our little cottage, which was all a bit strange because I didn't think anyone knew we were here apart from the Bartons and they didn't have a Range Rover. They had a whole garage full of cars, including Jake's Dad's absolutely gobsmackingly gorgeous Aston Martin DB9, but I didn't remember seeing a black Range Rover in there. Perhaps it was the owners coming back for something, or the people from the farm next door?

Chapter 9

Hojo held his microphone to the window pane and could hear the conversation quite clearly – a man's voice, a woman replying. Then he heard the man call to his second daughter to come and help his favourite son lay the table. He gave a thumbs up to the other two team members, followed by four fingers to indicate the number of occupants, pulled off his headphones and put away the microphone.

'Mother, father, son and daughter,' he whispered, 'all present and correct.'

Brutus knocked on the door and it was opened a short while later by the Professor, who thought it was his daughter and didn't really check who was there, so he just threw the door open.

'Professor Fenwick?'

The Professor blinked in astonishment at the three men crowded round the little cottage doorway. In fact, he noticed that the first one was already half inside.

'Sorry, you left the door open, so I assumed it was OK to come in?' came the smiling introduction from Brutus.

'Yes, do come in out of the cold. Sorry, I thought you were someone else – what can I do for you?' enquired the somewhat confused Professor.

At that point the Ransack team, who had quietly been spreading out and checking who was in the cottage, drew their guns.

'Just sit down on the sofa over there with your wife and daughter and I'll let you know.'

The Professor was about to correct them as to it not actually being his daughter, when his wife silenced him with a look, and he realised that announcing there was another person to be kidnapped or threatened or whatever was not a good move. This was not the time for his usual pedantry.

'What do you want, we have no money, and this is not our house?'

'All will become clear in a minute, Professor.' Chuck and Hojo came back into the room, dragging John with them, who was kicking and screaming and shouting 'get off me, you wanker!'

'There's no-one else, except this one who keeps calling me a wanker, whatever that means?' and he threw John onto the sofa. 'Go and sit next to your sister, you rude little jerk, and don't say another word!'

John looked at his Mum and Dad in total confusion, but they just put a finger to their lips and made ssshhing noises. The fact that there were four coats, and four pairs of hiking boots standing right by the door had obviously convinced the gunmen that they had the Professor, his wife and two children. Whilst Brutus covered them with his gun, Chuck and Hojo came over and put plastic cuffs on Gudrun, Susan and John and taped their mouths shut. John tried to resist and they simply knocked him out cold and then bound and gagged him to the horror of the others. Brutus pointed his gun at them and in a very quiet menacing voice told them not to move.

'Right, that will keep the rest of you quiet whilst I talk to the Professor here. OK, first question, who were you expecting just now?'

The Professor thought hard – he couldn't say it was his daughter as they would then capture her as well, so he came up with an idea quickly. 'Oh, I thought you were the neighbours coming over for a drink – we met them earlier and thought they might pop in.'

'How far away are these neighbours then?' asked Brutus whilst studying the champagne bottle and four glasses. Luckily there were only four glasses standing there as Susan didn't like champagne.

'They are in the farm you passed at the end of the drive – you came left up to us, right goes to the farmhouse.' Thank God he was observant and had spotted all that as they drove in, the Professor thought. Brutus waved to Chuck to check the window and the view to the neighbours, and Chuck gave a thumbs up.

'No car outside and the windows all closed – looks like they've gone out,' he reported.

'Right, Professor Fenwick, one nice easy question – where is the prototype for the fuel cell system?' asked

Brutus as he helped himself to a glass of champagne.

The question burst into the room like a bombshell as the Professor didn't think anyone knew he had a successful prototype.

'I d,don't have any successful p,prototypes yet,' he stammered and looked at his wife for reassurance. His wife, however, looked rather uncomfortable, and he couldn't work out why, and then it hit him. His wife had told someone he had completed his research and was obviously trying to get money for his work.

'You didn't?' he mouthed at her and she hung her head in shame.

'So, Professor, you didn't know that the little woman had tried to make some money from your endeavours? Interesting! Yes, your wife very kindly gave us details of your exploits and told us the four of you were going away for a little break this weekend. Handy things cell phones,' he said, holding up his own, 'we just tracked your wife's cell phone and voila, we found you. Anyway, what that means is that we know that you do have a successful prototype, but I am sorry to disappoint you, Mrs Fenwick – we have no intention of paying for it.'

The Professor's wife looked at him in shock, as the reality of the situation slowly began to dawn on her.

'You probably think your little prototype and other bits and pieces are all safe in the hands of your lawyers – so sorry, we intercepted that parcel last week. But, I'm sure you kept a copy of everything for yourself, didn't you? No, Professor, you wouldn't send off something as important as this and not keep a copy.

Maybe not the prototype itself, but at least all the information needed to manufacture it and how to store the hydrogen. We've searched your house down in Surrey and we found nothing there, so you must have brought it with you?'

He looked across at the Professor and his wife, who were looking more and more ashen with each revelation, and the Professor had moved away from his wife as he couldn't face the fact that her betrayal had brought them into all this danger. 'So, I'll ask you just one more time, Professor, where are the workings? I will happily take this cottage to pieces to find it, but let's save some time shall we? What's on this laptop?' Brutus picked up the laptop and tried to look at the contents, but the screen-saver had come on and it was locked.

The occupants of the sofa looked shattered, as their whole world came tumbling down around them. A few minutes earlier they had been laughing and joking, and now they had three hoodlums waving guns around, planning to steal the Professor's most important work. The Professor's wife was pleading with her eyes to make her husband tell them what he knew, and Susan was looking absolutely terrified.

'Well,' started the Professor as he frantically tried to come up with a clever strategy, 'as you rightly say, there is nothing at home, as I removed it all before we came up here, and there is nothing here so don't bother looking. That's my daughter's laptop and we were simply looking up where we are going hiking tomorrow. Why don't you tell me what you, or your

American masters, are going to do with my work if I tell you what you want to know?'

The Professor was watching Brutus's face closely and he saw the quick flicker of surprise as the American barb hit home. Brutus had been working hard on his British accent, and he thought he could pass for a Brit.

'What makes you think I am paid by the Americans?'

'Firstly,' started the Professor, who always resorted to pedantry when he felt stressed or panicked, 'there are very few Americans who can do a convincing British accent, as proven by Dick van Dyke in Mary Poppins and yourself especially when you use words like cell phone – we call them mobiles. Secondly your colleague does not appear to know what a wanker is – a very common English expletive, for which the American equivalent would, I believe, be jerk. As Oscar Wilde so correctly pointed out years ago, we are two nations separated by a common language...'

'SHUT UP!! I DON'T NEED ANY FUCKING LANGUAGE LESSONS FROM SOME LIMEY FAGGOT!!!' screamed Brutus, who had steadily been losing his temper during the Professor's tedious explanation, as he pistol-whipped the Professor. The pain was awful, and blood started to stream down from the cut on the Professor's cheek. One tooth appeared to have come loose as well as he felt round the inside of his mouth with his tongue.

The Professor's wife and Susan tried to scream behind their gags, and the Professor balled his fists as if he were about to strike someone in retaliation, but fortunately realised the futility of any such action. Meanwhile, he kept a pained expression on his face as he didn't want the thug to see that he was secretly slightly happy, as he had obviously started to get under the American's skin. Also he had just seen his daughter's face duck away from the window, so he knew she was safe for the moment and keeping the Americans' attention on himself would stop them from looking out of the windows. If his daughter was safe, then there was still a route to his fuel cell work open via the caches – all was not lost.

'Oh congratulations,' he croaked through a mouthful of blood, 'another startling display of how Americans think that everything can be settled by beating the shit out of people, using guns or invading their country.' He thought that would earn him another swipe, but the American obviously had to keep him alive for the moment. 'So, as I was saying, what are you going to do with my work if I tell you what you want to know?'

'Oh, come on, you are a *clever English Professor*,' he taunted making quotation marks in the air, 'so I am sure you can work it out?' Brutus settled himself in one of the armchairs and looked down to check his shoes hadn't got any blood on them.

'Well, to be honest, there are several options, and I would be interested which one you have in mind. You could patent it, sell it to the highest bidder, franchise it?'

Brutus shook his head, 'Come on Prof, you can do better than that.'

'Well, you told me you've intercepted the prototype and the documentation I sent to my lawyers, and now you want the only remaining copy of the workings.'

No way was the Professor going to tell them that there was yet another copy hidden in the cache for his daughter, as he thought through the implications of what he had learnt.

'Oh God, you are going to destroy it, aren't you?' Brutus nodded. 'But that's a criminal waste, and the planet will be ruined by all the carbon emissions, and millions of people will die.'

The Professor's vision of hell on earth was opening up before his eyes. He looked across at his wife, with an *I told you so* expression on his face, and reached out a comforting hand to Susan.

'Yes, Professor, but if you happen to be sitting on some of the largest oil deposits in the world, you would probably think a bit differently?'

The professor nodded glumly. He straightened his back, smiled at his wife, son and second daughter and then looked up at Brutus.

'I rather thought you might say that, so here is a message, in your vernacular, to you and your Arab or American or whatever paymaster, GO FUCK YOURSELF MOTHERFUCKER!' and that did earn him a thorough beating, until Brutus was pulled off by Chuck, not without some difficulty and not in compassion, but to ensure that Brutus didn't kill him. Brutus looked furious when he saw blood on his suit.

'OK, Professor, let's try this another way.' As the Professor's jaw dropped, and his wife's eyes said *sorry*,

I never thought it would come to this, Brutus grabbed Susan by the hair and forced her to her knees on the floor.

'How would you like it if I cut up your daughter's face, or let one of my men have a quiet intimate session with her? Tasty little piece of ass, as we Yanks would say.'

Tears were pouring down Susan's face and she was pleading for help. The Professor's wife was squirming with frustration. Susan wasn't the Professor's daughter, but he wasn't going to tell them that, and how could he possibly let anybody suffer, whether they were his own flesh and blood or not.

'Leave her alone, that won't be necessary.'

Brutus smiled. He simply let go of Susan, and let her fall to the floor. He looked at the Professor with an enquiring look. 'Ah, beginning to see things my way are we Professor?'

'Yes, you seem to hold all the cards, but I still want to know one thing. What is going to happen to my family and myself if I tell you?'

Brutus grinned evilly. 'Well, Professor, I could have threatened to hurt your family if you ever worked on the project again, but that is so time consuming, and I like closure on my missions. I didn't really want to hurt your family as they are pretty unimportant to me. I hear you like little puzzles, so here's how I solved this one. I set up a very neat little plan, and it started SO well with intercepting the package for your lawyers. I had hoped to find all the workings at your house. That part is unfortunately incomplete, but I do believe we're very close now. So despite your having disturbed my plan, I believe I am close to getting it back on track. Oh yes, and then we left you a little surprise in your piano. The next time you played it would be BOOM, goodbye Professor, and no more working on a replacement – rather sweet don't you think?' and Brutus took another sip of champagne as he toasted his own brilliance.

The Professor looked totally sickened by the prospect, but that had rather unpleasantly confirmed his suspicions that his staying alive was obviously not part of their plan, which totally pissed him off. He just hoped he could at least save his wife, John and Susan. And the one thing the gunmen still didn't know was that he had another copy hidden in the caches. He wasn't going to tell them that and the only other person who knew about them was Angela.

'All right. You have the prototypes and no-one here apart from me knows where I have hidden my documentation.'

He knew this had effectively just signed his death warrant, but he might be able to save the others.

'I don't care what you do to any of us, I will not divulge the hiding place under any circumstances,' and as he finished the sentence he leapt from the sofa and grabbed for Brutus's gun.

The fact that he was being attacked at all by a nondescript English faggot Professor caught Brutus by surprise for a moment and it enabled the Professor to get a hand on the gun, but Brutus's superior strength soon turned the weapon back towards the Professor, who at that point tried desperately once more to get the gun away from Brutus. The sound of the bullet froze the room, and then the rest of his family looked terrified as they saw the Professor slumped on the floor, obviously very much dead.

Shit, thought Brutus, he had been looking forwards to roughing up the Professor a bit, and the daughter looked quite tasty. Yet again he was having to amend a plan due to the Professor's interference, and now he had witnesses to a killing. Well, in his heart of hearts, he had always expected to have to clear up all the loose ends, and now he had a perfectly legitimate excuse. His first move was to knock out the wife and the daughter so they couldn't interfere with any of his plans and then he turned to Chuck and Hojo.

'OK, one dead Professor, and no trail to the prototypes – that will keep the Sheikh happy. Grab the laptop as I don't trust the Professor. Let's torch this place so it looks like an accident. I DO NOT WANT any witnesses. Let's close the windows and put the gas on – Hojo, one of your little incendiaries should do nicely.'

He had told the Sheikh right at the beginning that simply eliminating the Professor would be much easier, but the Sheikh wanted to ensure that everything was destroyed. And that was what Brutus was going to tell him.

Chapter 10

As I turned the corner into our lane, I could have sworn I saw one of the men from the Range Rover hide a gun under the back of his jacket. What the hell?

I crept along the ditch to the cottage and sidled up next to one of the windows as quietly as I could. I sneaked a peak in and saw three men with guns, and my Mum, Dad, brother and Susan sitting on the sofa. I think my Dad saw me as I quickly ducked away, but was ninety-nine percent sure no-one else had. Round the back I thought as that door is locked and they won't come out there in a hurry. There was a big keyhole in the back door and I knew the key wasn't in it as John had locked it when he came back in from picking the beans and hung the key on the hook on the wall. He's neat like that. I groped in my pocket for my mobile phone to call the police and realised I had left it in the cottage - shit.

I alternated between looking through the keyhole – I

would have laughed at that if I hadn't been so bloody petrified – and putting my ear against it to hear what was going on. Then I realised that the kitchen window was slightly ajar, so I could hear enough that way whilst keeping my eye to the keyhole.

I heard the big black guy say he was going to destroy Dad's work, which was really going to piss my Dad off, and then Dad swore at him, which was either very brave or very foolhardy – the latter judging by the reaction he got. Ouch, you bastard! Next I heard that the package he had sent to the lawyers had been intercepted, which meant only the laptop and the cache were left, and the laptop was lying there in full view – shit and double shit! How the hell did they intercept the one Dad sent to the lawyers? The bastards, that really screws Dad's chances of negotiating – perhaps he'll give them the laptop and keep quiet about the cache?

Then the big black guy grabbed Susan and threatened to *'cut up your daughter's face'*. I wanted to shout that Susan wasn't Dad's daughter; I was outside here you bastard, but that wouldn't have been very bright. It also took a moment for me to twig that if they thought they had me in there, they didn't know about Susan. That also meant they didn't know I was out here. It was all very confusing. This was like one of Dad's bloody logic problems - no-one is looking for me, they think Susan is me, ergo they must think they have the whole family, ergo I need to keep my head down. Poor Susan, she only came because her moronic boyfriend dumped her and now some thug is threatening to cut her face, because he thinks she is me.

The pistol shot nearly made me wet myself and I had to stifle an involuntary scream. I looked through the keyhole and saw Dad slumped on the floor, and the three gunmen were bashing my Mum and Susan on the head to knock them out. You vicious, cruel, despicable, sodding bastards – that's my Dad you just shot and my family and best friend you are bashing about. If there hadn't been a solid door between me and them I would have been in there like a shot tearing their eyes out. Which, of course, would have been stupid, as there were three of them with guns and just little old me, but I was so angry I swear I could have taken all of them at that moment.

I put my eye back to the door to see what was going on, and I heard the instructions to close the windows and torch the place. No, you can't do that, that's evil. Just take the laptop and get out of my life – let me go in and see if my Dad is alive and help Mum, John and Susan. However, I could smell gas coming through the door and common sense took over from emotion for a moment and I decided it was time to run for my life.

I crawled away along the wall until I was clear of the windows, and then sprinted as quickly and quietly as I could behind Dad's car. It appeared that they were so engrossed with burning down the cottage, that they weren't looking outside, which was pretty bloody lucky. One half of me wanted to get away as far and as fast as I could, but how the hell could I leave Mum, Dad, John and Susan to burn to death? I had to find a place to hide till the bastards went away and then see if I could save my family.

Chapter 11

The Ransack team closed the cottage door and walked casually to the Range Rover, as they didn't want anyone to see people running away from the cottage.

Hojo had set up a simple timer on an incendiary device next to the gas hob, which would go off in a couple of minutes' time – another selection from his little box of tricks – and with the gas left on, the cottage should be nice and full of gas by the time the incendiary kicked in.

With the satisfied feel of a job well done and a bonus earnt, the three of them climbed back in the car and drove off to a hill a mile or so away, where they could watch the cottage and check that their plan had worked.

As they drove up to the top of the hill they heard a muffled explosion in the background, and when they parked the car and looked back they could see flames flickering round the cottage.

    Brutus smiled. Mission accomplished, or as that English faggot would have said 'Job done, old chap'.

Chapter 12

As soon as the gunmen left, I shot across to the back door and frantically tried to open it. I didn't want to go round the front as I wasn't sure how far they had gone and I didn't want them to see me. Open, you bastard door, open. Liz would have been shocked at the things I was doing to my nails. Who cares about nails, though, you can regrow them - you can't regrow a family. Come on, you stupid bastard door. I could not shift it at all, that's the problem with these old buildings, they are built properly. Dad would have liked that, he approved of things being built properly.

I couldn't get to grips with him being dead, with my whole family being dead, I had only seen them a short while ago laughing and .... stop it, I'm going to burst into tears if I keep going down that track.

I frantically cast around the garden for anything I could use to smash the door or a window. The tools were all locked away, the car was locked and the windows had double glazing. I remember someone telling me double-glazing was hard to smash in, which is why windows had to open far enough nowadays for you to be able to jump out of in the case of a fire. Amazing what goes through your brain when you are in a total state of panic.

I tried to dig a rock out of the ground, but just got bloody fingers and even more ripped nails. THINK, THINK! I wanted to scream for help, but I couldn't do that – Christ, the frustration was killing me. God, I know I've ignored you a bit lately, but could you possibly hand me a crowbar?

I had a quick look through the kitchen window to see if anyone was stirring. Nothing. Then I spotted a funny timer type thing sitting on the gas hob. Christ, only five seconds left. I ducked down – don't ask me why, it just felt safer that way, after all it was a properly built cottage and the walls should be thick enough to protect me?

Then I heard a click inside, a blast rocked the cottage and a great sheet of flame blew out part of the back door. Well, I wanted it open, but not like that - my family was still in there, and they must have turned the gas on, the bastards. I tried to get in through the hole in the back door, but there was thick smoke and flames billowing everywhere and I couldn't get in. How can a fire spread so bloody quickly? You never believe it when they show you on the TV, but now I knew they were right.

So I sat there hunched against the wall, bawling my eyes out, trying to get to grips with the loss of my family and the sheer frustration of not being able to do anything about it – there wasn't even a tap or a bucket. Then suddenly it hit me. They think we're all dead. If the neighbours and the fire brigade comes now, they will find me and the gunmen will know I am still alive, and they will come back and kill me. My answer to the logic problem said that they thought they had all four of us, and hence they now think we are all dead, ergo no-one knows I am alive. One more look through the window and all I could see was flames and smoke.

Oh shit, get out of here.

But where do I go?

Get in there and save your family.

I can't get in!

Shit, this was tearing me apart.

Taking the car wasn't an option. I hadn't got the keys and that would have told the gunmen that someone was still alive. A quick look over the hedge and I could see the neighbour's car had gone, so they weren't there, which meant I would have go down the lane to the village and probably meet the gunmen – no good. My only hope really was that the police come, find four people (I couldn't bring myself to say bodies yet) and that is what would be reported in the papers. At least then the gunmen would think they had killed us all. How sick is that, my best friend dying when it should have been me?

All these thoughts were zooming through my brain and it was hard to get any real conscious thought or planning in place. I just knew that I had to get away, so I started walking out through the woods at the back where no-one could see me. I kept glancing back trying to convince myself that there was no way I could have saved any of them, but I kept thinking there must be something I could have done. That thought and the picture of the burning cottage were going to be my personal hell for a long, long time.

*

I knew there was a village over the back about a mile away, as we had seen it on Google Earth when looking up the caches. Just get there was my first and only thought and then you can decide what to do.

As I walked along I felt in my pockets for a tissue, because my face was a complete mess with mascara running down my cheeks. My mobile was back in the cottage, which was a pain, but then I remembered all those thrillers I had read where the baddies trace the good guy, because he makes a call or turns his mobile on. I've no idea if it's true but they all say that it's as good as a homing beacon. So perhaps not the end of the world after all.

After half an hour or so I found the path down to the next village. Now, please, give me a phone box that works, I prayed. At least up here vandalism shouldn't be such an issue, you would have thought.

I wandered through the middle of the village trying to look as if I belonged there. Fortunately at this time of year, there were lots of tourists about, so another strange face wasn't going to concern them. Then I spotted the phone box, between the church and the pub. I had worked out who I was going to phone on the way here – obvious really. The person, who had helped me out of all sorts of scrapes for years.

Jake.

Chapter 13

Only problem as I got to the phone box is that I realised I had virtually no change with me – I had used that to buy the cream, which I still had in my other pocket. How the hell could I phone Jake now?

My first reaction was to quit the idea of phoning Jake and simply dial 999 instead. The problem was that on the walk over here I had convinced myself that I shouldn't contact the police until the story had appeared in the papers saying that we were all, well, ... dead. That way I thought it would lull the gunmen into a false sense of security. Knowing the way the press seemed to stick its nose into everything that is happening, and blasting it across the front page with total disregard for the people involved put me off the idea of contacting anyone just yet. Dad had had a run-in with the police and the tabloids a few years back and they were not his favourite people.

I forced myself back to the present and tried to get a

grip; there had to be a way. In the back of my mind was something Dad tried to tell me about ages ago when he was explaining that he had lived in a world without mobile phones – couldn't really see how that would ever work? Anyway, he said that in the old days, you could call people and make them pay for it, which is the part that had appealed to me! Oh yes, I suddenly got it, all I had to do was reverse the charges.

So I dialled the operator and in my best, if somewhat shaky, phone voice asked if I could make a reverse charges call. Much to my surprise she took that as the correct introduction and asked me for the name and number. Then she asked for my name. Despite my paranoia, I couldn't believe anyone was tracing this call, so I gave my real name. I also asked the operator to say it was an emergency, and that I would repay Jake when we met up as I knew he would think it was all a joke or a bit of a cheek otherwise. A few seconds later I could hear her asking for a Mr Jake Barton.

'Yes, this is Jake Barton.' Hooray, he was there.

'Will you accept a reverse charges call from a Ms Angela Fenwick?'

'What a bloody cheek. Tell her no.' I tried talking down the phone, but then I realised Jake couldn't hear me yet. Must be a system where they only connect you when he says yes.

'She says it is an emergency, and she will repay you when you meet again.'

'Oh, all right then.'

'You may carry on now Ms Fenwick.'

I wanted to shout all of my problems down the

phone to Jake, but thought I had better check the operator wasn't listening in – I wasn't really sure how this reverse charges thing worked, and paranoia was my middle name by now. Angela Paranoia Fenwick. Nervous wreck and blithering idiot.

'Operator, are you still there?'

'No, it's me Jake, what the hell are you up to?'

'Just a second Jake .... operator?....' nothing. 'Oh Jake, I'm sorry but ... oh where do I start .... they killed him ... and I couldn't save them .... oh God it was a nightmare,' and I burst into tears and slid down the wall of the telephone booth clutching the handset in desperation to my ear.

'Angela, are you there, Angela? You are making no sense – are you all right?'

The joy of hearing a friendly voice. I couldn't talk for a moment.

'Angela, this had better not be some sick joke?'

'Jake,' big gulp, 'this is not a sick joke. Dad is dead – they shot him.'

The next few minutes were not the most coherent of my life, but eventually Jake managed to get the bare bones of the story from me. I also told him I had had to run away and was now in a little village in a phone box between the pub and the church. He asked why I didn't simply call the police, and I told him it was all very complicated and that wasn't an option just at this moment, so please don't tell anyone about this call. I didn't want anyone to know I was alive at this moment until I had got my head round everything that had happened.

God bless him, my guardian angel said he would climb in the car and be there as fast as he could. Liz had gone home as she had a busy day tomorrow (hair, nails and shopping were my immediate catty thoughts), so he was kicking around the house bored anyway.

I told him I would be in the pub or the church. As it happens, it was the church as I hadn't got enough money to sit in the pub and I didn't really want anyone looking at me and remembering me. Probably a blessing in disguise, as I am sure I would have tried to drown my sorrows in a big way, and that would not have been a pretty sight.

Chapter 14

'Well done Brutus, that seems to have cleared up any loose ends. Your bonus has been transferred. Let's hope that is the end of this tedious affair.'

The Sheikh put the phone down. He wasn't really a sheikh, of course, but that fool Brutus thought that all *A-rabs* were to be despised unless they were someone special, so he chose the name to shut the stupid American up. It also helped to put him off the track, were he ever to be foolish enough to come looking for him. He doubted it, as Brutus enjoyed his regular payments and bonuses too much, but the Sheikh didn't get where he was today without being careful.

He had spent years and millions covering his tracks very carefully. To the outside world, he was simply a very successful businessman, who could be relied upon to get the appropriate people to the bargaining table. That was how he had heard of the possible hydrogen storage breakthrough, through one of the

American government officials he had had dealings with. To a very, very small group of people, however, who held the same beliefs and would lay down their lives for him, he was probably the leading terrorist in the world.

He looked at the contents of his desk. Such a small device, but such huge implications. He had told Brutus that he was going to destroy the prototype and all the workings, which was of course absolute rubbish. One day the tide would turn, and his region's dependence on the oil reserves was not going to be sufficient. When that day came, he was going to have the salvation ready for the planet, and he was going to sell it for billions to the power-hungry nations. But, he would make the accursed Americans suffer dearly and pay the most. He was sure the Prophet would approve of such a punishment for such a heathen race.

There was no point in simply destroying their buildings like Bin Laden had done. In the Sheikh's opinion that just promoted sympathy for the enemy and anger for the perpetrator. Oh no, the way to attack America was through its wallet. He had made a killing on the stock markets with 9/11, because he had heard that a major attack was due. That had been a sweet moment, and he wanted more of them. He had carefully been planting seeds round the world, and every now and then one of them blossomed – a run on the bank in the UK, a rogue trader in France. These people were so desperate in their daily chase for money that they had exposed themselves dramatically. The world markets were in turmoil as the banks were so greedy and had simply lent money to people who could never afford to repay it. Unbelievable, and he had quite neatly helped that crisis along by dropping some ideas into senior bankers' heads about repackaging and selling on their toxic debts. In their greed for bonuses, they had needed little prompting.

The Americans and many others in the West were quite simply the greediest pigs on the planet. Allah, in his infinite wisdom, had given his people oil. The Americans, of course, did not have enough oil for their own needs, and their greed prompted them to trample over other nations with no regard for their people or their heritage. Invade Iraq because of Hussein? What a fatuous excuse! If the world truly worried about despotic tyrants, then they would have removed Mugabe and Kim Jong-il years ago. It was only ever about feeding their insatiable hunger for oil. No, the Americans hated it, but Islam had the oil, and now he had the replacement for it. That fool Bush talked about the axis of evil. No, that was not the answer, we are the axis of oil, and that meant the axis of power. Praise be to Allah.

*

A knock on the door interrupted his thoughts, and his brother Mansur entered. They had adjoining suites at the Savoy. He might despise the West, but he could see no reason to live in discomfort, and their service was simply excellent. Mansur means *divinely aided, victorious,* and that was how he and Mansur saw their war against the heathens.

'The contents of the laptop are excellent. Some of the files were encrypted, but the American was clever enough to keep the laptop running and we could extract the keys from the RAM memory. I am sure we will be able to exploit them for the good of Islam when the time is ripe...'

'I detect some concern, my brother, what is it?'

'There are a lot of files on the laptop to do with hiding things and setting puzzles to find them. I am concerned that the Professor hid a copy of his work and it may turn up.'

The Sheikh's eyes took on a harsh glare.

'Show me', he commanded.

'There appears to be some strange sport the Professor is addicted to called geocaching. It seems that people hide little treasures – not real ones, just plastic boxes – and others try to find them using their GPS devices. I would have ignored it as just a game, but there is one file which talks about hiding *a USB stick with all the relevant documentation in a cache* and letting his children find it as test.'

'Well, the children are dead, so there should be no problem?'

'Yes, but the geocaching website is public and hundreds of people are out there searching - what if someone finds this USB stick?'

'Well, we will just have to find it first. If this USB stick truly exists, then we must have it. Mansur, I entrust you with this mission as it needs brains, rather than brawn, and in that department you are certainly the most gifted of us all.'

He used the obnoxious Brutus and his team for the *wet* jobs, but he certainly did not trust the monstrous American brute. To him, it was a fine piece of irony that a group of Americans were helping him to destroy their country without realising it.

'Keep me updated on progress on a daily basis – we cannot fail.'

'As you command, Hashim, my brother.'

Hashim. Destroyer of evil.

If the Professor had put something or someone in his path, he would quite simply destroy it and them.

Chapter 15

I heard the door of the church creak open. I was hiding in the organ loft, as the last place people tend to look when they come in somewhere is above them – another fact from my Dad, which I had thought was useless at the time. God, how I missed him, and why did I ever argue with Mum and John – it all seemed so petty now. I heard footsteps, and a voice called out.

'Angela?'

I waited to see if he was alone and then in a stage whisper I said, 'Jake, up here, I'm coming down!'

I flew down the stairs and into his arms, shaking and sobbing and basically letting everything go that had been pent up inside me for the last few hours. Jake looked somewhat concerned, but I think he realised that he wasn't going to get any speech out of me for a while, and Mutt was circling us in total confusion.

'Come along, you're frozen, come and warm up in the car.'

'Are you alone?' Little Miss Paranoia was still alive and well.

'Yes, of course, who else apart from Mutt and me would drive up here for several hours? I told you Liz had gone home... you really are terrified aren't you?'

'TRY WATCHING SOMEONE SHOOT YOUR FATHER AND THEN SET FIRE TO THE REST OF YOUR FAMILY AND BEST FRIEND AND THEN NOT BE ABLE TO ANYTHING ABOUT IT AND THEN NOT EVEN BE ABLE TO BREAK A WINDOW OR ...'

Jake grabbed my arms and shook me. 'Sorry, you were heading towards hysteria there.' He folded me into his arms and stroked my hair. 'You've had a terrible time, which frankly I can't really understand.' I nodded feebly, and let the tears stream down Jake's fleece.

'It's not your fault that this...dreadful thing.. has happened.' Jake tilted my face up and looked me in the eyes. 'Look, as I understand it, if you had tried to save them, you would be dead yourself.'

I had realised that at the back of my mind, but it needed someone to say it out loud before it really sank in. Jake passed me a pack of tissues as I was a blubbering wreck and then he asked me again why we couldn't just contact the police and hand everything over to them. I told him about wanting the story in the paper first. I am not sure he was totally convinced by my logic, but I promised him I would contact the police as soon as the papers said I was... dead. Sounds easy now, but it took me a long time to get that word out loud.

Now I needed rational though to set in, so that my family and best friend hadn't died in vain. I seemed to remember that someone once said that revenge is a dish best served cold, well stuff that, I wanted it piping hot.

Chapter 16

'Chief, we have bodies in here, four of them'.

The fire brigade had managed to put out the fire, and the cottage was now a pile of smoking rubble. They were picking their way through the remains for the one thing they didn't want to find – bodies – and the one thing they did – the cause. Probably a chip-pan fire or something equally stupid. When will these people learn to be responsible and fit smoke alarms? The Fire Chief hated chip pans.

As the Chief called in the ambulance service for the grisly job of removing the four bodies, another of his men called him over urgently. In the wreckage were the mangled remains of what looked suspiciously like a timer near to the remains of the gas hob. Not a kitchen timer, but a far more suspicious looking bit of scrap. That combined with the strange positions the bodies had been found in – almost as if they had their hands tied behind their backs – convinced him something very wrong was afoot.

'Right, that changes the whole complexion, everybody out now, and we get the inspectors in. Jones, get them on the blower, I'll call the local CID.'

DCI Jenkins was just settling down in front of the television when the phone rang. A suspicious fire at a remote cottage was all he needed to make a perfect evening! Apologising to his wife and telling her not to wait up, he climbed in the car and drove over to meet the Fire Chief and his inspectors. On the way over he called his scene of crime and forensic people to give them the low-down. He didn't want to ruin their evenings, but the Fire Chief suspected arson with four unidentified bodies. It was going to be a long night.

As he drove along he rattled off a series of calls to his team, setting up enquiries to find out who the cottage belonged to, where the nearest neighbours were, where the bodies had been sent to, when he could expect the post-mortem results, a trace on the registration of the car parked outside the cottage, and all the other paraphernalia of what he feared was the beginning of a murder investigation.

The car registration came back very quickly – a Professor Fenwick from Surrey. So he fired off more calls. Contact the Surrey police and see if the Professor is at home. A short while later and his mobile rang. The Professor's house had been broken into and the burglars had got away with a bunch of stuff, including PCs, assorted electronic kit, and it also looked like a safe had been ripped out. According to the neighbours, only the water board had been round whilst the family had been away, which made DCI Jenkins curious, and he told his people to get on to the water board and find out why and when they had been there.

Well, his guess was that The Professor was in the cottage, and people had burgled him whilst he was away. There was a bitter irony in there somewhere.

Chapter 17

As we drove down the motorway, Jake asked me why anyone would want to kill my Dad. I suddenly realised that in all the chaos of getting away, and getting help I hadn't actually got round to telling him what this was all about.

'Jake, my family and Susan have been killed for what you want me to tell you. Do you really want to know what this is about?'

'Angela, I've known you since you were two, and we've shared secrets for as long as I can remember. Now I've driven hundreds of miles to rescue you, so I think that all entitles me to know what is going on.'

'Jake, it's not about trust, it's just that I don't want to put anyone else in danger.'

'Well, I'm sorry to bring a touch of reality into the equation, but you probably can't go home as you don't want anyone to know you are alive?' I nodded agreement.

'You probably don't have much money on you and you can't use credit cards or cash machines, as they can trace that; you can't use your phone as that's gone – should I carry on?'

'No thanks, I think that's enough depression for one night!' I said with a wry grin.

'Ah, that's a start,' said Jake, 'that's the first bit of humour I've had from you tonight! So are you going to let me help you or not?'

I didn't want to suck Jake into this mess any further than I already had, but I couldn't really see how to avoid it. However, I wasn't going to tell him everything now, so I agreed to let him listen in when I explained everything to the police. Maybe another example of not being totally rational, but I felt that if the police knew about it all then telling Jake as well was not so dangerous.

We got back to his parents' house in the early hours of the morning. He told me that we would obviously have to say something to his parents in the morning, as he had simply said to them that he had to go out and help a friend when he left, and not to worry as he would be home late. So we crept in quietly and Jake showed me to the guest bedroom upstairs, where Susan and I had slept just a short while ago. I was fine till I saw the bed where she had slept, and then I just seemed to fall apart.

'Jake, I'm s,sorry, but I can't sleep alone – that's where Susan was last night. Can you sleep over there?' Jake looked a bit confused. 'It's just that... I just need someone to be there?'

Jake nodded and told me to wait whilst he got a couple of things. He came back holding a pair of old pyjamas for me to change into whilst he went to the bathroom, and told Mutt to look after me. I was just dropping off when he came back, and I felt him plant a little kiss on my cheek. I wondered what Jake wore in bed, but I was simply too tired to look.

In fact, I slept like a log and didn't wake up till half way through the morning. Mutt wagged his tail and gave a quiet woof and I patted the bed for him to jump up and have a cuddle. Jake appeared a few minutes later with a cup of tea and a little wash bag.

'Thought I heard you two. Here, this is one of Dad's airline freebies from all the flights he does; it's not wonderful but at least it has a toothbrush and stuff in there. Dad's gone to work, so it's just Mum downstairs, and I've told her that you're here and that you've had a traumatic shock, but she doesn't know any more than that yet. Shower, bathroom, loo are all next door as you know. Help yourself and come down when you're ready - OK?'

I nodded. I could get used to seeing Jake first thing every morning. All going well, I'll find out what he wears in bed another day. Amazing, I never knew that you could still think about sex when you were in a state of shock. Must be that Maslow pyramid thing we did at school. I seemed to remember that the bottom layer was all about breathing, excretion, food, water, sleep and sex, so he seems to have been spot on. Safety was the next layer and I was getting there gradually and after that was love and friendship, which must be why I automatically thought of Jake I suppose.

The shower was a joy – I felt as if I had sixteen layers of dirt everywhere. Somehow I was trying not only to get clean but to also wash away the pain and guilt of last night. That was going to take a long time, but once I had cleaned myself up and got dressed I felt miles better. I must get some clean clothes, and my nails were an absolute disaster. Please God, don't let Liz see them, as she would probably come over all faint! That's better, I thought, my sense of humour appears to be returning, I feel strong enough to start the day.

There was nothing in the morning papers, so we watched the lunchtime news, and there it was – *Four killed in mystery fire at cottage*. It was really weird to see it scrolling across the bottom of the screen. Normally you vaguely register what the writing says, but now I was a major part of that story and every individual word seemed to knock me sideways. I have the feeling I stopped breathing for a while and wasn't aware of anything else happening in the room.

It was even worse when there was a short clip of a police inspector standing next to the ruins of the cottage saying that the cause of the fire and the victims' names weren't confirmed yet. I just gazed numbly at the smoking ruin, knowing that Mum, Dad, John and Susan had died in there due to some evil bastard. Jake got the policeman's name though – DCI Jenkins.

It took me quite a while to get through to the right police station, but the magic words *cottage fire, I know who the victims were* got me through to DCI Jenkins. They also seemed to be very interested when I told them my name was Angela Fenwick.

Jake leant over and pressed the speaker-phone button with a *may I?* on his lips. I nodded, as that was going to be much easier than relaying everything. I felt like I had climbed to the ten-meter diving board and was about to jump off.

Here goes, I thought.

'DCI Jenkins here, Miss Fenwick, I hear you have some information for me in relation to the cottage fire in Ireby.'

'Yes, I do, because only by sheer luck did I avoid being one of the victims myself.'

'Why is that?'

'Look, let me start at the beginning. My Dad rented the cottage for a short break for us four, and my best friend Susan.'

'Your father is Professor Fenwick?'

'Yes, how did you know that?'

'His car was parked outside the cottage, Miss Fenwick. And who are the other people?'

'Sorry, so that's my father, Professor Harold Fenwick. He rented the cottage for a holiday for all of us. The others are... or rather were, my mother, my brother and my best friend Susan Mortimer.' This was not getting any easier. Telling it just brought back images of flames and smoke.

'Take your time, Miss Fenwick, and just tell me what happened.'

'We arrived there a couple of days ago. Last night,

just before dinner Mum sent me out to get some cream from the local shop.'

'What time was that?'

'It was about 6.30. Anyway, as I came out of the shop I nearly got knocked over by a black Range Rover tearing through the village. Next minute I saw it turning up our drive, which was weird as no-one knew we were there, so I thought it might be the owners coming back.' That bit was easy, now came the tricky part. 'As I walked up the lane I saw one of the men from the Range Rover hide a gun under the back of his jacket.'

I then continued explaining how I had peeked through the window and seen three men with guns, and then listened at the kitchen window whilst looking through the back door keyhole.

'That's when I saw the big black one shoot my Dad.' Jake's mother gasped. 'The next thing I heard them say was that they were going to *"torch the place"*, so I hid till they drove away.' Another gasp from Jake's Mum, who looked as white as a sheet. 'I tried to smash the window or get the door open but I couldn't get the bloody thing open, and they were burning ... inside ... and I couldn't help them and ...'

I was sobbing down the phone by this time. I heard his voice trying to speak to me and I simply handed the phone to Jake.

Jake chatted to the Inspector whilst Jake's Mum came over and gave me a huge hug and calmed me down. Eventually I got my act back together and reached for the phone again.

'Sorry about that.'

'No need to apologise, Miss Fenwick, you appear to have had a very traumatic experience and I am sorry to have to make you relive it. You have to appreciate though, that is all a little strange from my point of view, and you have raised a lot of questions.'

I started answering all his questions. I even told him I still had the pint of cream in my jacket pocket from the shop, all of which I hoped would begin to convince him that I was a victim and not some crazed daughter trying to do away with her parents. Fortunately I am annoyingly observant, so I told him the registration number of the Range Rover, and that got him very excited; I could hear him rattling off commands to someone to look up the registration number.

The most difficult part was when he asked me why I had run off, rather than waiting for the fire brigade to arrive. I tried to explain that at that particular moment I was terrified for my life, and the thought of hanging around was just not an option. I had also convinced myself that following my plan the gangsters would end up hearing that four people had died, and hence wouldn't have any idea that I had survived. We went round it a couple of times, and he grudgingly admitted that it made a weird kind of sense, especially when I took him round the logical conclusion I had arrived at about the gunmen thinking Susan was me. Why else would they threaten to cut the daughter's face? Dad knew I was outside, as he had seen me at the window, so they must have all been protecting me.

'Mum and Dad have always called Susan their

second daughter, as she is, ... sorry was ... virtually part of the family. I can only assume the gunmen heard that and thought,' gulp, 'they had me.'

'Which brings me to the key question, Miss Fenwick, why would anyone want to murder your father?'

'My father had just finished designing a brilliant new device worth billions and they wanted the prototype and the details of how to manufacture it. He had sent a copy to his lawyers, but they intercepted that and now they wanted to make sure there weren't any more copies. He wouldn't give it to them, because they said they were going to destroy his invention, and Dad said he couldn't allow that.' I paused, and took a deep breath because this was the bit that would haunt me for life. 'So he threw himself at the gunman and that's, ...that's when the bastard shot him.'

And that was all I could manage for the moment, so I handed the phone to Jake once again and collapsed in a heap on the sofa. Jake's Mum grabbed me and we both started crying our eyes out.

Jake gave him their address and asked for the police to come round as quickly as possible, because they were all now thoroughly terrified by what they had just heard.

Chapter 18

Aunt Janet was hugging me to her ample bosom and was still crying almost as much as I was.

'You do believe me, don't you? I tried, I really tried, but I couldn't save them. They were the worst two minutes of my life.'

'Ssshhh, of course we believe you darling, there is no way you would ever let anyone harm your Mum and Dad. You loved them to bits; and your brother and Susan – I just can't believe it. You poor angel, it's a monstrous crime that anything like that should happen.'

'There is another problem,' I managed to get out between the sobs.

'What's that, dear?'

'Well, what on earth do we tell Susan's parents? They need to know that Susan is d...dead, but how on earth can I ask them to not tell anybody and keep it quiet?'

'Let's discuss that with the police when they come, Angela, as they probably have more experience with all this sort of thing than we have. I know that's not a great answer, dear, but I think we need all the help we can get right now – OK?' I nodded glumly, as to be honest I couldn't really face talking to anyone else right at that moment.

Jake in the meantime had made a cup of tea. What would we do without tea? We all sat there in a bit of a daze and you could see Jake and his Mum were desperate to ask more questions. I asked them to please wait till the police got here, as I didn't really want to have go through it again and again.

There was a discrete buzz – the police had arrived at the security gates (I told you the Bartons had money). Gosh, the police really could get there quickly if they needed to. Jake went and let them in. A couple of minutes later I could hear voices in the hall and then Jake ushered them into the family room.

'Mum, Angela, this is DS Smythe and WPC Robbins, please do sit down. Anyone for tea?'

Nods all round and Jake's Mum sent him over to hold my hand whilst she made more tea for everyone.

'Right, Ms Fenwick, we've heard the basic details from our colleagues, but we would like to take a full statement from you now please?'

Lead on I thought, and with a deep breath I ploughed in and told them the whole story from start to finish. Well, to be honest, not quite the whole story. I did remember some other details like the timer on the gas hob and the big black guy saying something about *"that will keep the sheikh happy"*, but I still hadn't told anyone about Dad hiding the USB stick for me to find. That was my secret for the moment as I had promised Dad I would use its contents properly. I had no idea how I was going to do it, but I knew I was going to find that cache and then broadcast the contents to the world at the Eco-Conference Dad had been talking about. I just hoped and prayed that all the tricks he had used were enough to throw the gangsters off the trail. I'd worry later about how I was actually go about finding it when a band of gunmen was after me, but hey one thing at a time.

I was off in my own little world of vengeance interspersed with flashbacks of the cottage, when I suddenly remembered the piano.

'Don't touch Dad's piano!' I screamed, and they all looked at me as if I were mad. 'They said they had put a bomb in Dad's piano, because they had planned to simply blow him up that way.'

DS Smythe grabbed the phone and started getting through to the Surrey police, and I could hear snippets about Bomb Squads, but I couldn't relax until I heard everyone was OK. I couldn't stand the thought of someone else getting blown up before I managed to warn them. A couple of minutes later he looked up at me and smiled and told me not to worry, as the house was cordoned off and the bomb disposal people were on their way.

Part 2 – The hunt

Chapter 19

The statement took a long time. Everything had to be written out longhand, and they put it in their strange police jargon. Then the WPC read it all back to me to check it was right, whilst her colleague went off to make some phone calls. After a while he came back and passed me the phone, saying it was DCI Jenkins again. I put it on the speaker again.

'Miss Fenwick, I just wanted to let you know that we have several witnesses, including the girl in the shop who remembers you, who saw the Range Rover. Unfortunately the registration number actually belongs to a sheep farmer up in Scotland, who hasn't been out of his village in the last three months. It would appear that your villains chose a number that couldn't be traced back to them. We have also found the remains of the incendiary device that was on the gas hob, and our specialists are looking at that. Last but not least the bomb squad found a very nasty booby trap in your father's piano.'

All round the room faces were looking more and more concerned. Uncle Bill had returned by this time and he couldn't get to grips with someone killing his best friend and his family. He was nursing a very large whisky as he was of the opinion that tea simply wasn't strong enough for this sort of tragedy.

'We are pursuing several lines of inquiry and we will obviously keep you informed. Now, what I want to discuss is where you are going to stay. You obviously can't return to your parents' house, and I want to ensure your safety.'

Uncle Bill immediately started saying that I could stay with them as no-one knew I was here and the whole place was behind secure gates and had burglar alarms. I took a deep breath and could see it was time to let out the next bit of information.

'Sorry, that's very kind, Uncle Bill, Aunt Janet, but there is one slight problem,' I said looking at them all. I'd been thinking about the USB stick and how the hell I was going to find it. I could hardly set out by myself, for all the reasons Jake had drummed into me on the way home last night, but I needed to at least get close to home to help work out the clues. Who was going to assist me in my quest was something I hadn't worked out yet, but I needed to at least start the process off.

'My father told me just before I went out to the shop, that he had hidden a copy of his work in a place near our house, that only my brother or I could find. I want to find that copy and make sure that my family and best friend did not die in vain. I need to find it and let the world know about it at the conference at the end of the month, where Dad was due to present. Do you have somewhere safe for me down in Surrey, DCI Jenkins?'

That, of course, threw the cat straight amongst the pigeons, with people saying that I should tell them where to look and they would do it for me and lots of other ideas. Trying to explain to them that I didn't actually know where it was, and that Dad had set a series of puzzles that I had to solve, which were based on things that only I knew all sounded very far-fetched, but Jake looked at me and grinned.

'That is so typical of your Dad, he was always setting tests and games for us when we grew up. Mealtimes or a trip in the car were never a simple time, he always had some mental game for us to play.'

That may sound hideously clever, but we loved it as Dad combined games with his silly sense of humour. One of his absolute favourites was the radio show *I'm Sorry, I Haven't a Clue* on Radio 4; proper comedy in his opinion, rather than *the claptrap and vulgarity that modern comedians think is funny.* We would play games where you have to come up with silly new definitions of words like *Barbeque – hairdresser's snooker equipment*, or *Parsnip – vasectomy,* or the one we all loved playing, which was *Late Arrivals at the ....* For example *Late Arrivals at the Dinner Table* could be *Mr and Mrs Ning Table and their daughter Di*. The worse they were, the more we laughed. Jake used to love them, and you could see the steam coming out of his ears as the cogs whizzed round in his brain and he tried to come up with a better (worse?) one than

Dad.

DCI Jenkins told us all to stay where we were and promised to call back as soon as possible. He requested the two police officers to stay there as protection in the meantime, which rather dampened the atmosphere for a while as we all thought of the implications of someone trying to find me and murder me. Also, before he rang off I raised what for me was a deeply important issue – namely getting hold of Susan's parents and telling them what was going on. Much to my surprise, and also to my great relief, DCI Jenkins had thought of that and had already sent a plainclothes officer in an unmarked car to both her Mum and her Dad to break the news and explain the need for total silence for the moment.

'They are both still there, waiting to hear my further instructions. Am I right in saying that effectively you want us and them to keep the lid on your being alive, and hence your friend Susan being dead, until the Conference at the end of the month?'

'Yes, I know that's a hideous thing to ask Susan's parents, but I honestly think that would be the safest thing all round.'

'In that case, Miss Fenwick, we had better find this USB stick pretty quickly, or life is going to become a whole lot more complicated than it already is.'

Too darned true I thought. Dad would almost have been proud of the complexity of the whole situation. I just wanted the whole thing to go away and be able to return to a normal life, although life was never really going to be normal ever again.

'Miss Mortimer's parents are deeply shocked, but obviously have no wish to put you in any sort of danger, so they have agreed to keep quiet for the moment. If anyone asks, they are simply going to say that Susan has gone off for a holiday to get over the break-up with her boyfriend. Now, can you let me talk to DS Smythe again please?'

DS Smythe picked up the phone and wandered away round the corner for a private conversation. God, what a mess. Poor Susan's parents. They couldn't even grieve for their daughter properly because of what those evil bastards had done to my family. The only thing that gave me hope and kept me going is that the swines who had killed my family did not know I was alive and all going well I had the means to bring their house of cards tumbling down. If I had known who was behind the whole thing at that stage, I probably would have fled to a desert island with Jake and never raised my head. Ignorance really is bliss sometimes.

I looked round the room, and I have never seen so many despondent faces in one place, except possibly a dentist's waiting room. This was getting us nowhere fast. If I sat there any longer, I would have to get out a Richard Ashcroft album and slit my wrists. Dad told me it was Leonard Cohen in his time - *music to top yourself by*, was Dad's opinion and having listened to some of the monotonous crap he turned out, I can see where Dad was coming from.

Time to snap out of it. So I smiled at them all and suggested we play a game of *Late Arrivals at the Computing Ball* (well, I wanted to look for a USB stick, so it seemed apt) as a small tribute to Dad. They all looked a bit shocked to start with, but I told them that it was what I wanted and that I really did think Dad would have approved. Uncle Bill smiled at me and said it was a brilliant idea and just the sort of thing Harold would have wanted in the circumstances.

Mr and Mrs NilComputer and their son Percy NilComputer was my first effort – I must admit I had been thinking about it for a while, so I was quite proud of my first attempt. Jake was a bit surprised that I could even think of anything amusing, but he looked in my eyes and could see a gentle plea there from me to try and forget the hell we currently were in. So he came back with *Mr and Mrs DeeDisplayPanel and their daughter Elsie DeeDisplayPanel,* which got a large thumbs-up from his Dad, who was always useless at this game, but loved listening to us play. We even got the police to join in - *Mr and Mrs RusSoftware and their Auntie Vi RusSoftware* from DS Smythe - and for me the winner from WPC Robbins was *all the way from China, please welcome Mr and Mrs Smat and their son Mao Smat.* She smiled at us all and explained that her Dad had been an avid fan as well, but most of the people down the station had no idea what she was talking about. I just hoped my Dad was up there looking down and listening, as it should have made him smile and it might have changed his mind about the police.

Chapter 20

'Jake, can I talk to you?' I wanted to get him away from the others for a few minutes. I smiled at the police officers and told them we were just going next door into the snooker room.

'Jake, you've been wonderful and rescuing me last night was absolutely brilliant, but I can't expect you to come down to Surrey. I need to go and sort this out by myself now.'

'Well, in the grand order of dinosaur droppings, that's the biggest load of crap you've come up with so far! Do you honestly think Mutt and I are going to stop now, when it's just starting to get interesting?' he leant down and patted Mutt's head. 'Do you really expect PC Plod to help you solve your father's puzzles? Come on, it normally took the two of us several hours, if not days, and a deep knowledge of your father's weird brain to crack his puzzles when we were younger.'

'But, what about Liz?'

'To be honest, she is a bit high maintenance, so I don't think it's going to last, especially as Mutt doesn't seem to like her all that much do you old chap?'

Mutt wagged his tail and slobbered all over Jake's trousers not understanding a word, but if that meant goodbye to Liz, then Mutt was the cleverest dog on the planet.

'To be honest, I'm basically bored rigid till I have to go back to Uni, we haven't got any gigs lined up, and I think Dad will let me stop the pub job and bung me a few quid under the circumstances. So how do we start? Do we have to go down to Surrey or can we start some of the puzzling here?'

'Are you sure? Really, really sure?'

'Shut up!' another big grin. 'Being serious, I think your Dad would be upset if I didn't help you. I shared his concerns for the planet; in fact, I think any right-minded person does now. So if he has truly come up with something to stop all this bloody pollution and stop our dependence on fossil fuels, then it would be a crying shame, if we didn't do our level-best to find it and share it.'

'Oh Jake, you are gorgeous!' and I grabbed him and gave him a big huge smacker on the lips. Caught him a bit by surprise, but he didn't object.

'OK, we need your laptop and an Internet connection,' I said, thinking ice broken on the kissing front, but don't push your luck too far just yet.

We returned to the family room to let them know what we had decided. Aunt Janet didn't look ecstatic, but Jake told her this was a lot safer than some of his exploits at Uni, that she knew nothing about, and the police pointed out that they would be providing protection. We explained that we were going to try to solve the beginning of Dad's puzzles, and hence we were off to the den to fire up Jake's laptop and the family PC.

Once Jake had booted up both machines I explained that the first thing we had to do was go into the geocaching website and find the caches that Dad had hidden for us. Fortunately Jake had done a couple of caches with us a year or so back, before they moved, so he knew the basics of the whole thing.

'So what nickname does Dad use for himself when he is geocaching?" Jake asked as people don't use their own names so as to retain some anonymity. Always struck me as slightly strange as they put all sorts of info about themselves in their personal profiles and once you contact them they all knew one another's real names and telephone numbers. They all meet up at least once a year in the pub, and Mum and Dad had been round to some of them for dinner. Go figure.

'Dad used to call himself *TheMadProfessor*, which wasn't wildly original, but it made him laugh!'

'OK, let's do a search on all the caches hidden by *TheMadProfessor* then."

'Sorry, too easy, Dad has put a few tricks in to make it more difficult to find.' I then explained that the first trick was that he had put the cache in under a different name with a different profile.

'Well, how are we going to find that, because you told me there are hundreds of cachers in the UK?" Jake asked very reasonably.

'Well, I've been thinking about that and there are a couple of things to help us along. First of all, he said it would be a name that John and I would recognise. No idea what that means yet, but it should help. Secondly he told me that the cache is set up in such a way that no-one except us will find it.'

'How did he manage that? Clues that only you know or what? And I thought the location was on the website anyway?'

Jake looked totally confused, so I repeated what Dad had told me about how puzzle caches work, and how he had cheated when setting it up by putting the wrong final location in the website. That way I explained, no-one could go to *Celo*, the man who checks them all, to get the location, and hacking into the website wouldn't help either. I could then see Jake's brain going down exactly the same path as I had with my Dad.

'Yes, but how the hell do we find them?'

'Ah, I'll tell you the next bit when we have found the listing. For the moment, I think we simply have to search for caches near our house, which haven't been found yet.'

'Don't we need an ID?'

'Not for the moment, anyone can search the website, but we'll probably set up one a bit later as it's free and gives us access to more info. Try thinking of a silly nickname for us.'

And so we started searching for caches near where we live in Surrey. We accessed the geocaching website, hit *Hide & Seek a Cache*, entered the postcode for my house and pressed *Go*. Over nine thousand caches found – bloody hell, I never really understood how popular this lark was. We looked closely and realised that was a hundred mile radius, so we tried again with just a ten mile radius. To say there were lots would be an understatement! Four hundred and twenty-three caches on twenty-two pages – ouch. There was one on the first page, not found yet, but it was placed today, so that couldn't be it.

'Shame you don't live in Monaco,' said Jake, 'there's only one cache there!'

'Ho, ho! Anyway, you are meant to be looking at Surrey, not Monaco.'

'Sorry, I was just trying listing by country. Let's see what the UK shows? Shit, over twenty-five thousand caches! You wouldn't have thought there were that many strange people with GPS devices around! What's this funny symbol on the left – it doesn't look like your normal caches or the puzzle ones your Dad liked?'

'Stick the cursor on it and it should tell you,' I leant across to have a look, 'oh, event caches, that's simply where they get together for a drink and a chat, it won't be one of those. Dad said it was a puzzle cache, so it will have a question mark on the left, and the middle column shows when it was placed, which must have been before we left home last Friday, so any date after that we can ignore.'

We both continued to search down the lists, but there didn't seem to be any caches that had been placed a few days ago that hadn't been found already. I had never realised quite how many active cache searchers there were. We found several recent ones, but nothing that smacked of my Dad.

'Right, stop a minute. We need to think laterally like Dad made us do.'

Dad loved to give us problems like this – *An apple and two pears cost forty pence; a pear and two apples cost thirty-five pence; how much do one apple and one pear cost?* We would all sit there frantically calculating the cost of an apple and doing equations in our heads and Dad would smile and say *no, think laterally*. The answer is that you actually add it all together and you know that three apples and three pears cost seventy-five pence, so one of each must cost twenty-five pence and who cares what each individual fruit costs? OK, an apple costs ten pence and a pear costs fifteen pence, but you don't need to work that out to solve the question.

'So, let's think about this a bit more rather than searching blindly. If it were simply a cache near where we lived that no-one had found, then it would be easy to see which one it is, right? We've tried that and it doesn't give us any.'

Jake nodded his agreement, 'So, it must have been found,' he looked at me for confirmation. I nodded. 'But no-one can find it,' he continued and then grinned as we both came to the same conclusion, 'except your Dad, so we simply look for caches he has found recently. Will it tell us who placed those?'

So we turned back to the PC and tried searching for caches found by *TheMadProfessor*. Hey Presto, a list of all the ones Dad had found, when he found them and who had placed them.

'OK, it will be a puzzle one, we can ignore the rest, let's see what we've got. Bloody hell, there are hundreds again,' I thought we were never going to find it, but then I realised that Dad had cached in lots of countries, so we could ignore all those, and a lot of the UK names were repeated. There were obviously a limited number of people, who actually placed puzzle caches round where we lived. A couple of pages more and then there it was in glorious black and white in the middle of the page.

'What did Dad always call me?' I asked Jake.

'Well, lots of rude names,' he replied with a cheeky grin as I tried to smack him,' but his favourite was some funny name from another of those Radio comedy series – let me think a minute.'

I turned the PC screen towards him and he smiled as he saw the name he was trying to remember: *grunt_futtock*.

'Yeehah, that's the one, give me a high five! Let's have a look at his profile and check if it's your Dad. No, that won't work, you have to be logged in, bugger.'

'No problem, I wanted to create an id and login anyway, so let's do that. What name have you thought of for us?'

'Well, I thought of *TheDesperados*?' I shook my head, '*Angels&Demons*?'

'Not bad, better book than the Da Vinci Code in my opinion, but I quite like the idea of *Haensel and Gretel* – it's German and they go off into the woods and get lost, so that seems apt!'

So Jake set up a new account and a couple of minutes later it was all ready to go. As part of the setup it asked for us an email id, so we simply set up a new one on Hotmail, which reminded me that Dad said he had set up an email for the *grunt_futtock* account. So I suggested that we have a look and see if there was an email account for *grunt_futtock*.

'Yes, but we need the password,' Jake quite rightly pointed out.

'Too true, but Dad said he had used his usual everyday password scheme. He had really good passwords for important stuff, but the rest of the time he just amused himself with a little scheme he used.'

'So what do I type in for the password then?' Jake asked

'Pissov' I replied

'Look, I'm trying to help, there's no need to be rude!'

'Sorry, couldn't resist,' I smiled, 'Dad used this scheme based on his so-called East European football team - would you please welcome the players onto the field? Pissov, Buggerov, Naffov, Sodov etcetera?'

Jake could hardly type for laughing, and pointed out that it was not the most politically correct thing he had heard in his life, but he quietly worked his way through the list and Sodov was the one we wanted. Bingo, we were in.

'Ah, there's one email here on hotmail from Dad? Let's have a look what it says.'

Well done, grunt_futtocks, you are on the trail, keep

*going. Don't forget to think diagonally, and it could be you finding the caches first! Do cod second.
Love Dad.'*

Ouch, I was gone again. Every time I was beginning to get my act together, something popped up and blew me apart. Jake came over and read my screen and simply knelt down next to me and held my hand.

'Don't hold back, Angela. Have a bloody good cry. There's absolutely nothing to be ashamed of. If I had lost my parents, I would be a complete gibbering wreck. I think you are being brilliant.' That was it, I was gone for the next few minutes, but I also promised myself that I wasn't going to lose Jake. The boy, sorry the man, was a rock, and if we came out of the end of this whole thing safely I was going to do my utmost best to hang on to him. I sat there crying my eyes out with Jake's arms round me and Mutt's face on my leg and let my rage and grief consume me.

After a while I had regained my composure, Jake quietly handed me some tissues to repair my face, and we got back to the task in hand.

'Right,' I sniffed in an effort to sound controlled and business-like, 'I'm not sure I understand all of that email, but knowing Dad it will come clear as we go along. Have a quick look at *grunt_futtock's* profile to check we are on the right track, because Dad said the hobbies would be totally wrong – what's it say?'

'Rock climbing, scuba diving and free-fall parachuting! That couldn't be further from your Dad if it tried. Your Dad is terrified of heights, and I seem to remember he nearly drowned as a child, so hates going underwater?'

'Spot on. Dad hated water. He was all right on top, so he did sailing and water-skiing when he was young, but he hated being underneath the water. When we were learning to swim, he pretended not to be afraid, so that we would learn properly. He was so relieved when we learnt to swim like fish, because then he could stop pretending and get us to save him if he got out of his depth!'

I could picture my Dad in the water looking very unhappy. Mum told me that soon after they met in Germany, she had taken him swimming at the local pool. Mum was a real water baby, and loved mucking about in the water, so she pulled him underwater as a joke and he bloody near killed her.

'All right?' said Jake, interrupting my memories. I nodded. 'It also says that he speaks fluent German, French and Italian. Is that true?'

'Well, Dad spoke fluent German as you know, but his French was pretty lousy and his Italian was about three words from memory, so that must be a red herring too. What else have you got?'

'*grunt_futtock* only has two caches and they are both puzzle caches, which only one person has found, namely .... drum roll ... *TheMadProfessor.* I do believe Doctor Watson that we are hot on the trail of the famous Moriarty.' Jake was pretending to puff on a pipe and was doing a pretty awful impression of Sherlock Holmes, but it made me laugh. 'So let's look what the puzzle is that the archfiend has left us,' puff,

puff, 'there are two caches under *grunt_futtock's* name. One is called *There's no F in Greece*, rude man, and the other one is called *About Time*. Which one do we start with then? The email said do cod second – there's no cod here.'

Jake looked at me in amazement as I groaned and then burst into laughter. 'You mean there's no f in cod?' I asked him, and he told me there was no need to be rude.

I had to explain to him that it was one of Dad's terrible jokes about a man, who went in to the chippy to buy cod and chips and was told there was no cod. The customer got very upset and asked how you could possibly have a chippy without any cod. The owner tried to calm him down and asked him quietly what you would get if you took the P out of Plaice? The man answered Lace. And if you took the S out of Skate, what would you get? Kate, replied the customer correctly. And if you took the F out of Cod? But there is no F in Cod, said the customer and the owner replied that that was what he had been trying to tell him for the last five minutes!

'Hey, it's not my joke,' I said, 'but at least we know where to start – *There's no F in Greece* comes second so we start with *About Time*.'

Jake fired up the cache page and we looked at it together. I explained to him that in puzzle caches, you had to look at everything – the title was a clue, the attributes might be a clue, the dummy coordinates were a clue sometimes, and so on and so on.

'OK, attributes are there on the right and they seem

to be as mad as the hobbies, scuba equipment needed, snowmobile, boat, climbing equipment, mine shafts, poisonous snakes – think your Dad was having fun. But what the hell are dummy coordinates? Now I'm totally confused – what are those?'

'When you publish a cache, they have to have a set of coordinates associated with them. On a normal cache, that is where the cache actually is – OK? But, on a puzzle cache, the people have to work out where the cache is, so the coordinates on the page point at a place that is a clue or are just some random spot vaguely near where the cache is. Where are the coordinates for the *About Time* one?'

It transpires my Dad had been fairly boring with the dummy coordinates.

> *The cache is not at the above coordinates - it's a garden centre with nice plants.*

He was spot on, I knew the garden centre well, as we had spent many weekends stocking up the car with shrubs and bulbs and things there. Which meant the title was probably the clue, so we looked at the rest of the page.

> *At twelve o'clock noon, the hour and minute hands of your watch are directly over one another. How long till that happens again? Write the answer as A hours, B minutes and CD.E seconds. The cache is at N 51 AB.CDE - West you'll have to work out somehow.*
>
> *If you want to waste some time, try working out*

when all three hands are directly over one another again, but that has nothing to do with the solution to this cache!!

'Well, that's easy,' I said, 'it's five past one, so 1 hour, 5 minutes and no seconds.'

'Sorry, Doctor Watson, it is not that elementary,' said Jake.

I looked at him in confusion – well at least I was doing the Doctor Watson impression right!

'Take your timepiece, young Watson, and wind it round to twelve o'clock. Have you managed that? Now, wind it slowly forwards to five past one. Pray tell me, are the aforementioned hands now directly over one another again, or is there indeed a small gap to be seen between them?'

'No shit Sherlock! The little hand has moved forwards a bit towards the two, so it must be a bit after five past one. How do we calculate that, you know I'm not very good at maths?'

'Well,' said Jake Holmes, who only needed a deerstalker now for me to want to permanently throttle him, 'you can do a simple mathematical calculation of how far each hand has moved after M minutes. The big hand will have moved a complete revolution and a bit, whereas the little hand, that's the one on Mickey's nose on your watch Watson,' I picked up a cushion and threw it at him, 'has only moved a bit. However I'll wager a pound of shag that there is a simpler way if your father set the puzzle!'

We were both giggling at this stage. I personally

quite fancied a pound of shag from Jake, but that would have to wait.

'I'll have a look on the Internet whilst you do the lateral thinking as you're better at that than I am,' he finished his impression with a theatrical twirl and turned back to his laptop.

So whilst Jake Googled various combinations, I played with my watch. I had twiddled it once to get just after five past one, so I kept going. Just after ten past two had them lined up again, and then again at a bit after quarter past three. I kept twiddling and kept counting and got eleven times in twelve hours. That was a bit strange, I appeared to have lost one? So I did it again, and yep, it does it eleven times in twelve hours, which actually made sense now as the hour hand was catching up a bit every hour. I looked at Jake and asked him if he had got the answer?

'Hang on, one more link, yep got it. What have you got?'

'Twelve hours divided by eleven. I just kept turning the hands and it happens eleven times in twelve hours. What have you got?'

'One hour 5 and 5/11 minutes – same thing. Now, what did your Dad want? Hours, minutes and seconds. That makes 1 hour, 5 minutes and 27.27 recurring seconds, so A must be 1, B must be 5 and CD.E must be 27.3 seconds, so that gives us North 51 15.273? But what the hell do we do for West?'

We looked at one another in total confusion. It had been going so well, and now we had come to a halt. We looked at the second part with the three hands, but that appeared to be a total red herring, as it never happens again till midnight, so we could forget about that.

'OK, back to lateral thinking,' said Jake, 'what sort of number are we looking for?' I looked confused, so he continued, 'what sort of number comes up for West round about your house?'

'Good thinking, Sherlock, let's have a quick look in Google Earth ... here you go, the range is normally somewhere between ten and twenty round where we live ... hang on and the dummy coordinates were West 16 something, so probably middle teens.'

Jake looked pensive and started fiddling round with Google Earth.

'There must be a clue we are missing. The background picture is just a clock – that doesn't seem to help. What else can we look at?'

'One of the tricks is to hide things in the HTML source itself – Dad told me he sometimes puts in comments in white text or hidden when he's feeling really nasty, so have a quick look at the source and see if there's anything there?' Jake shook his head. 'Which leaves Dad's strange email and comment about *think diagonally*, which I thought meant tap on a brick like in Diagon Alley in Harry Potter?'

Jake suddenly leapt back into Google Earth and played round again.

'Dr Watson, I believe have a theory. What did Holmes always say – get rid of all the shit and what's left must be right?'

'I think he put it a bit more politely than that, but yes

that was the gist!'

'OK then, if you draw the line x = y as a graph what do you get?' Jake asked me and I told him to forget it as I never understood algebra or any of that stuff. 'All right, just believe me when I tell you it looks like this ...'

'A diagonal line,' I cried, 'so what the hell does that mean?'

'What it means, I think, is that we simply make North and West the same. That would give us North 51 15.273 and West 00 15.273 – now try that in Google Earth and see what on earth – sorry about the pun – comes up?'

'The good news,' I said, 'is that it is not far from the garden centre dummy coordinates, but the bad news is that it appears to be in the middle of a field. Mmm, not sure, have a whirl on geochecker and see what it says.' I had shown Jake geochecker before, and explained that you could check if your answer was correct.

Jake started giving me high fives 'Geochecker says SUCCESS! Whoohoo! Yipee! uh-huh, uh-huh! w00t! Yeah, baby! Now, go get it! So I'll take that as a yes. And, yes the map shows me the middle of a field, just near Pebblehill Road, which is only a few miles from your house, isn't it?'

There you go, Dad, cracked it already, hope you're proud of us I thought. Then it hit me, we hadn't actually found it, we had just found the wrong location, which Dad had put in there to throw people off the trail.

'Sorry to be a party-pooper, Jake, but that's the

146

wrong answer.' He looked crestfallen, so I tried to cheer him up, 'well, it's the right answer to Dad's puzzle, and you're very clever, but as I explained before, that's not where the cache is hidden.'

'Oh shit, I'd forgotten that bit. What do we do now?'

'Well, let's look at the logs of the people who have tried to find it.'

Not only do the geocachers write in the little logbooks in the caches themselves, but they also write up every found / not found on the website. Dad told me that they didn't always put the DNFs – Did Not Finds – in there as some of them didn't like to admit failure, but geocachers were a remarkably honest lot. After all, you could actually lie through your teeth and say you had found a cache even though you had never been there, especially on the small ones where there wasn't room for a pencil – *oh dear, I forgot my pencil* – but Dad didn't know anyone who did that.

After all, he would explain to me, the whole point is the thrill of going there and finding it. To him making up a find would be the equivalent of people counting their score wrong at golf – yes, you can do it, but you're only cheating yourself and no-one wants to play with you any more after that.

'Your Dad is the only one, who has found it, on guess when... April 1st, which also happens to be the date the listing was published, and he just says, *not obvious, but insider knowledge helped*, which makes sense when you know what's going on. The others have all posted DNF and are obviously none too happy. *Easy puzzle for North, but had to guess West;*

gecochecker says yes, but an hour's search revealed nothing; looked everywhere in a 100 yard radius and found nothing. Is this an April Fool's joke? Nothing matching the clue anywhere around. Looks like your Dad has achieved his objective, so how do we find it? Is there anything else you haven't told me yet, or anywhere else I can go and look?'

I was racking my brains to remember everything Dad had told me up in the cottage. We had looked at the hobbies, and yes they were rubbish, we had thought diagonally, we had got his dreadful joke about the F in Cod, but what else had he said, something about the bit he'd been proudest of? ... *The hints on the geocaching website will purposely be meaningless and misleading to other people, but should be meaningful to you and your brother. I must admit, that's the bit I'm proudest of, even if I say so myself* ... yes, that was it.

'Jake, what's in the hints section at the end?'

'Looks like gibberish to me – it just says *Senpgher*?'

'Hit the decrypt button next to it – they always encrypt the hints, so that you can try do the caches without any help, but I think we need all the help we can get!'

'Ah, that looks better, now it says *Fracture*, which was rather a good movie starring Anthony Hopkins from memory. Mean anything to you?' asked Jake expectantly. I shook my head as I had never even heard of it, let alone seen it.

Looking on Wikipedia we found there were actually two films, one made in New Zealand in 2004, and the one with Anthony Hopkins in 2007. We read through the entries for both of them and couldn't spot anything obvious, and I was a bit confused because Dad was not really a movie buff. He was always forgetting who was in a movie, or would fall asleep watching them on the plane and miss the middle or the end, so I wasn't convinced that he would use a movie as a clue, but I couldn't for the life of me think of anything that I had ever fractured. I had ridden bikes and ponies and fallen out of trees, but never broken anything.

Another of Dad's frustrating clues, that were obvious once you got there, but meaningless beforehand. Stupid me, I had thought we could just breeze down the motorway, pick up the cache, and that would be that. Robert ist dein Onkel. You see, all that education was not wasted. Should have known better as Dad's puzzles were never that easy. There was a call from the kitchen to come and help, so Jake suggested we should have a pause and let the others know that we had at least made some progress, which made a lot of sense. That way we could pick their brains as well and see if they came up with any inspiration.

Chapter 21

'Ah, we wondered where you two had got to. Jake, can you go and help your mother lay the table please whilst I have a quiet chat with Angela?'

Uncle Bill came over and handed me a large glass of wine, explaining that it was medicinal. I sat down next to him on the sofa, where he gently explained that he and my Dad had a handshake agreement that they would look after one another's kids if anything ever went wrong, so I was not to worry about anything for the moment except helping to find the killers and solving the caches. I nodded my thanks, and told him that to be honest I hadn't really thought about anything beyond that for the moment as I was so tied up in trying to solve Dad's puzzles.

'Fine, leave everything with Janet and me and shout if you need us for anything – OK? Now, where have Jake and you got to?'

So slowly but surely I took him through what we

had worked out so far. He didn't really understand all the strange geocaching stuff, but he loved puzzles and was happy to check through our logic and our conclusions. He started ticking them off on the fingers of his left hand.

'OK, *grunt_futtock* was from one of your father's favourite radio shows *Round the Horne*, and I've heard him call you that many a time. I get the bit about no F in cod; he told me that dreadful joke years ago! The hobbies and attributes appear to be a bit of a red herring, but that is what your father was trying to achieve with that part, so I think we can ignore them for the moment. The clock puzzle is typical as your father loved lateral logical type things.' Bill reached the little finger,' and last but not least the diagonal part makes a lot of sense, although I would never have got it. John would have cracked that the same way as Jake probably as they both love maths, which leaves me with no fingers and the strange clue about *Fracture* if I've got it right?'

'Yes, that's what we've got so far and I really don't think it's about movies.'

'What about the second cache, the one about F in Greece or whatever?'

I nearly spilt my wine as I hit myself on the head and called myself *special*. We had been so tied up in the first cache we had forgotten about the second one. I wanted to rush off to the PC again immediately, but Uncle Bill insisted that we sat down and had dinner first as Janet would go ballistic if all her cookery efforts were ignored.

'Have no fear, we will all apply our minds to it after dinner. I am getting into your father's brain now and we will see what we can extract from this sea of confusion. Judging by the wondrous smells coming through from the kitchen though, I think the time has come to gather our friends from the police and go through to the dining-room. With any luck they will be on duty and won't be able to drink any of this rather good wine. I know John had the better palate, but would you like to hazard a guess where this comes from?'

Well, one thing that John and I had listened to over the years was Dad talking about wine, as it meant we got to taste it as well. I held up the glass, which I hadn't really been concentrating on till then, looked at the colour and then took a deep sniff and a healthy slurp. I rolled it round my mouth and remembered some of the things Dad had taught us over the years.

'Southern hemisphere, oaked chardonnay?' I asked tentatively.

'Your father would be proud. Coonawarra, South Australia. I chose something with a bit of body as Janet tells me the starter is full of garlic!' Bill beamed with pleasure and put his arm round my shoulders as he led me to the dining-room, where Jake was just putting out the starters.

Clever old Uncle Bill had made me think about something else and Aunt Janet appeared to have pulled out all the stops. I was desperate to get back to the PC, but I also realised that I was starving as I had only been picking at food all day, and grilled tiger prawns in garlic butter as a starter got me very interested. The main course was a gorgeous Beef Wellington, because Aunt Janet knew I liked my beef to walk off the plate, and that reminded me of another of Dad's dreadful stories about the uncouth person being asked how he liked his steak, to which the reply was *cut off its horns, wipe its arse and slap it on the plate!* With that one we had a very fruity Chilean Merlot - magic.

Aunt Janet could see we were desperate to get back to the puzzles, so she told us we could take our pudding through to the den and pick up where we had left off. Uncle Bill took command as he was used to running business campaigns and to him this was an exercise in marshalling his resources. He made me look at the location in Google Earth again to see if it rang any bells, but I explained that it was a place I had never been to and wasn't on any of the paths or bridleways we had used. We had never really ventured down the bottom of the Downs on our walks, as we had places like Headley Heath, Walton Heath, Box Hill, Reigate Hill and many others all on our doorstep.

Having exhausted that approach, he then moved us on to the second cache, and with nervous anticipation I opened up the cache page to find a typical Dad puzzle called Fibonacci numbers:

The original problem that Fibonacci investigated (in the year 1202) was about how fast rabbits could breed in ideal circumstances. Suppose a newly-born pair of rabbits, one male, one female, is put in a field.

Rabbits are able to mate at the age of one month so that at the end of its second month a female can produce another pair of rabbits. Suppose that our rabbits never die and that the female always produces one new pair (one male, one female) every month from the second month on. The puzzle that Fibonacci posed was... How many pairs will there be in one year?

Jake was about to launch into working out the problem, when we realised that my Dad had actually given us the answer!

OK, now the good news - the answer is a very famous series. The number of pairs of rabbits at the end of each month is 1,1,2,3,5,8,13,21,34,55,89,144 etc. If you haven't come across them before, each number is the sum of the previous two.

These are known as the Fibonacci numbers, and they have some fascinating properties.

1. *Try dividing each one by the previous one. Start from the left and work to the right. Are you beginning to home in on a number?*
2. *Try dividing each one by the following one and adding one - same number?*
3. *Get a calculator. Type in 1. Add 1. Do 1/x (the reciprocal). Add 1. 1/x. Add 1. 1/x. Keep repeating. What number do you get?*
4. *Calculator again - type in 1 add 1. Take the square root. Add 1. Square root. Add 1. Square root. Keep*

repeating. What number do you get?

Write the number down as A.BCDEFGH
North is 51 AB.(CDE+FGH). West is another matter.

Jake dished out a couple of calculators and we all started doing the calculations. Much to our amazement we all seemed to be coming out at the same number, which wasn't actually that surprising as Dad wouldn't have set it if it didn't work. The number appeared to be 1.61803 something if we had done our sums right. Jake in the meantime was doing some Google searching on Fibonacci, as it said it rang a bell with something he had learnt at school, and a couple of minutes later he turned round and beamed at us and asked if 1.61803399 was any good. I did a few more repetitions on my calculator and nodded. Uncle Bill said he had the same and we both looked at Jake to ask where he had got his number from.

'Believe it or not, you have just worked out the number Phi, otherwise known as the golden ratio.'

'What's that, when it's at home?' I asked.

'It's a very famous ratio used in art and architecture to layout buildings and things it says here, and was used in the Parthenon, the Great Mosque of Kairouan, and by people like Le Corbusier in his work and Da Vinci in the Vitruvian Man; that's the famous picture with the chap with his arms and legs sticking out. Why would your Dad use that?'

'I think you will find it was your father's interest in

photography that did it,' said Uncle Bill, 'he tried to explain to me several times how you should lay out a photograph and not have the horizon or the main subject simply sitting in the middle as that was boring. From memory, they call it the rule of thirds nowadays, which is not quite accurate, but near enough. The other neat thing that has just occurred to me is that Phi is the letter F in Greece – hence the title of the cache. Clever.'

We turned back to the cache a page and looked what we had to do with the numbers we had.

'Your father says to write it down as A.BCDEFGH, which gives me 1.6180340 if I understand him right. 180 + 340 gives 520, so that gives us a North value of 51 16.520, which seems reasonable as that's near your house. West he says is another matter.'

'Do you think there's any chance he used the same scheme as the last one, with North and West simply the same, as he kept telling me to think diagonally?'

Jake turned back to geochecker and gave it whirl, 'Yep, yeehah, success...and now we just need to see where is it on Google Earth...and the answer is, oh dear, another field and this time it is in Headley?'

I looked at the screen as Jake zoomed in and it was a field that I had never been to in my life as far as I was aware. And that was it apart from it being set and found on April 1st again and another one-word hint saying *Rocky*, which started up the whole conversation about movies again.

We were getting absolutely nowhere when the front gate buzzer went again. DS Smythe explained that it was probably the officers designated to take over from them and went with Uncle Bill to answer the intercom and check who was there. A couple of minutes later an extremely scruffy-looking individual and a young woman in smart jeans and a lovely tailored leather jacket appeared in the dining-room.

'My apologies for being a little late,' the scruff began in an accent which didn't really match his appearance, 'but the traffic on the motorway was hideous. My name is Terry Watkins, my colleague is Christine Wallace and we are here to provide protection for a Mr Jake Barton and a Miss Angela Fenwick,' and he looked round the room studying each of the occupants carefully before finishing with a smile for me. 'I know this is all a bit confusing at present, but we are running round like mad to try and understand what is going on, and in the meantime I am here to make sure that Jake and Angela don't come to any harm. I also apologise for my appearance, I have literally just come off another job, which required me to *blend* in with the surroundings. Mr. Barton,' he looked enquiringly at Uncle Bill, 'could I ask you to show me round the house and the garden before the light goes totally? Christine will stay here with the family while we look around.'

Aunt Janet explained that there had been a flurry of telephone calls whilst we were trying to solve the caches, and they had been told that two protection people would be arriving during the course of the evening. Christine nodded and told us not to worry, and was sure that Uncle Bill would explain everything when he came back in as he had been talking to the police and other agencies for ages. Jake and I looked at one another in surprise. It was lovely to be looked after so well, but it all seemed to be happening much faster than we had expected.

Chapter 22

A short while later Uncle Bill came back in with Scruffy, and I could hear them discussing burglar alarms and gates and outside lights. Scruffy seemed reasonably happy and asked Aunt Janet if he and Christine could dump their sleeping bags in one of the bedrooms. She told them not to be silly, as they had lots of rooms and she would make up a couple of beds for them later. She would have done it straight away, but like the rest of us, she was intrigued to hear what was going to happen next.

'I can see you are all desperate to understand what is going on, so Mr Barton, if you would like to start with what you learnt in your various phone calls this afternoon, Christine and I will fill in the rest.'

Uncle Bill gathered his thoughts, 'It would appear Angela, that your father was rather better known in Government circles than even I had realised. He was apparently a member of a couple of think-tanks that I knew about, but was also involved in a far less well-known and very secret committee. They haven't told me what that was all about, and frankly I don't think we need to know, but what it means is that your father's tragic death has triggered off all sorts of panic in the corridors of power. Now the good news from what you have told us is that the gunmen didn't appear to know about your father's other role and were just interested in his work on the fuel cell and the hydrogen storage. However, when you were telling us about the big black guy in the cottage, you told us you heard him say something about *the Sheikh*.'

I nodded, 'Yes, he said *that will keep the Sheikh happy*.'

'And that is what I am told has got some people very interested indeed,' said Uncle Bill and turned to Scruffy.

'Yes, in a nutshell we have picked up the name *the Sheikh* being used in connection with several incidents, which are of particular interest to national security,' said Scruffy. 'I am afraid it is beyond my brief or my knowledge to tell you more at this stage, but I can tell you about the arrangements that have been made for you starting tomorrow.'

Scruffy then went on to explain that they would be driving us down to a safe house in Surrey early in the morning, where Jake and I would be based whilst we searched for Dad's caches. Christine would be my personal bodyguard and he would be Jake's. When we arrived we would be briefed by some of the people who had been on the phone this afternoon and I would be asked to look at a series of photos, to see if I could identify any of the killers.

'Any questions at this point?'

'Yes,' Jake and I replied almost simultaneously, 'can Mutt come too, please?' I smiled at Jake and continued, 'Jake hates being parted from him, but we also want him there because he was always good at sniffing out caches when we went hunting with Dad.'

Mutt knew that we were talking about him and he wandered forwards and stuck his cold nose into Scruffy's hand. Scruffy smiled at him and started to stroke the back of his head. 'I think we have just appointed a new member of the squad. Mutt, you are now officially the team mascot.' Mutt was so happy to find a new friend that his tail nearly fell off as he wagged it furiously.

'OK, folks, I suggest we all get to bed now as we have an early start in the morning.'

'Sorry, one other thing,' I piped up, 'I haven't got any clothes or anything – can we do a quick bit of shopping somewhere along the way?'

Christine smiled at me and said she would make sure we did that tomorrow. Uncle Bill told Jake to use his emergency credit card – apparently he had one for University that Uncle Bill had set up, but was not allowed to use it unless it was really, really necessary. Boys can live in grubby old clothes for a week, as Scruffy was proving – we girls need a bit more variety, so this was definitely really, really necessary!

Chapter 23

'I am not at all happy with my prime suspect swanning off down to the South of England on what may well be a wild goose chase!'

'Detective Chief Inspector, I can assure you that Angela will not be out of our sight the whole time. She will be staying in a safe house, which she cannot leave and her personal bodyguard will be monitoring every move she makes. I must admit I don't currently share your belief that she is a suspect, but whilst she is here she will be watched very closely indeed and if anything does not seem to be right, we shall call you in straight away.'

'Let me remind you, Mr Smith, that Miss Fenwick had the motive, an enormous amount of money, the opportunity and no real alibi. The Range Rover could be pure chance, and until I get some corroborating evidence I am not ruling her out of my investigation.'

'My dear Inspector, that is perfectly correct and you

would not be doing your job if you didn't work that way. May I also suggest that you are perfectly welcome to come down here and interview Miss Fenwick if that would help?'

Chapter 24

There was a knock on the door and Jake appeared with a cup of tea. God it really was early – ouch. I told him I would surface in a couple of minutes, shower and come down. Christine, who had been sleeping in the other bed, had obviously got up already. Packing wasn't exactly going to take a long time as all I had was Jake's old pyjamas and his Dad's freebie wash bag.

Downstairs, there was a stranger in the kitchen and I nearly screamed and ran out of the room before I realised that Scruffy had undergone a complete transformation. The clothes were neat and tidy, and the stubbly beard had disappeared. He grinned at me and explained that this was what he normally looked like. Jake appeared with a few bags, one for clothes, one for Mutt's stuff, and one with his laptop in.

Uncle Bill and Aunt Janet were obviously putting a brave face on it all, as they saw their only son and newly inherited ward about to disappear off on some strange and potentially dangerous adventure. They walked with us out to the car and there were some very tearful hugs and goodbyes. Fortunately Terry – I must start calling him that rather than Scruffy – had an estate car so Mutt and the luggage went in the back and Jake and I got in the back seat.

As we rolled through the gates off down to Surrey, Jake and I turned back to see his Mum and Dad clutching one another and waving goodbye. I just hoped the next time we saw them, it would be in rather better circumstances with big smiles all round.

Jake clutched my hand and made a brave face. 'Right, where are we going to buy you some clothes?' Good boy, take a girl shopping and she will cheer up immediately!

A few hours and a very satisfying shopping-trip later we rolled in through the gates of a rather imposing country house on the outskirts of Leatherhead. I could just hear Dad complaining that this was how his tax money was being squandered, but I don't think he would complain about his daughter being kept safe and sound. We were met at the front door by a friendly chap, who grabbed our bags and told us we were expected. He asked Terry to take us through to the library where all the others had apparently gathered whilst waiting for us.

For one dreadful moment, I thought I was in a dream and had suddenly been transported to some weird TV reality show, so I grabbed Jake's arm with my right hand and Mutt's collar with my left and marched off behind Terry, who had obviously been here before and knew his way round. Christine whispered to me that this was her first time here, and she was a bit overwhelmed too, so that made me feel a lot better.

As we walked into the library the buzz of conversation died away and five sets of eyes turned round to study us. A man in a pin-strip suit and hideous tie came over and stretched out his hand in welcome.

'Ah, you must be Miss Fenwick and this is Mr Barton I assume? I'm sorry, but no-one told me the dog's name?' he added attempting to put us at ease. 'Come in and sit down. You will forgive me if I don't actually introduce everybody formally, but any names we gave you would all be made up anyway! To make things easier simply call us Andrew, Bert, Charles, Donald and Edward,' he pointed at his colleagues in order round the room finishing with himself.

The five men all smiled at me as they were introduced, although I couldn't help noticing that Charles had difficulty keeping eye contact.

'You are probably guessing that certain agencies are represented here, and we only need James Bond to walk in?' We nodded and giggled nervously. 'Well I can promise you that all the people that matter are represented here, and are working with the highest authority, but I'm afraid I can't promise you Daniel Craig or Judi Dench! My colleagues are mainly here to listen, and if you simply address any questions or answers to me, that would be best I think. OK?'

This was getting more surreal by the moment, but at least he obviously liked Mutt as he hadn't stopped petting him from the moment he first met him. E for Edward looked across at us and asked if we would like anything to eat or drink before we started, and although I really wanted a stiff vodka, I voted for a large glass of water as I felt I was going to be talking a lot.

'Let me first say Miss Fenwick, or may I call you Angela? ... how extremely sorry we were to hear about the tragic death of your family and best friend. It is almost impossible to imagine the traumas you have been through and if we could spare you any more anguish, trust me we would; but I hope you agree that the best thing all round at this stage is to catch the perpetrators of this evil deed and bring them to justice?' I nodded my head furiously.

'Your father was an extremely valued member of a committee together with myself and some of my colleagues here and we know just how good a man he was. We also know that he had been working on what to him was probably the most important project of his life, and like you we would hate that work to be wasted. Now, can you take us through the events of that evening in the Lake District – we have heard the details second and third hand, but we really would like to hear it from the horse's mouth so to speak. We have heard that you have been working your way through your father's clues, and we will come to that later, but if I could prevail upon you to start at the beginning and work your way through that would help enormously?'

So I took them slowly, but surely, through the whole thing. They made me start right back at the beginning when I had invited Susan as they hadn't really understood the *second daughter* bit up till then. I worked my way through the drive up, staying with the Bartons, going on to the cottage, the walk up Catbells and then the evening where it had all gone pear-shaped.

'It all started with Dad calling us together to tell us about his new invention. He had been super secretive about it, and hadn't even told Uncle Bill, sorry Jake's Dad, about it. There was a bit of aggro with my Mum, because Dad wanted to give it away and Mum wanted to make lots of money from it, but Dad was adamant that something so key to the planet's future should be available to everyone.'

There were nods around the room, as they agreed that that was typical of my father, who always said he had enough money and that the planet was way more important than his buying a Ferrari and polluting it even more.

'That's when Mum got a bit shirty and sent John off to pick some beans from the garden, Susan was looking at the laptop and Dad called me over to explain about his caches.'

They asked me to keep the cache conversation for later as they wanted to get the cottage part of the story clear in their minds first. So I told them that the next thing was being sent out to get the cream and nearly being knocked over by the Range Rover. I had seen the registration plates, but apparently they had been nicked from some poor bloke up in Scotland. The next part was getting slightly easier with each telling of it, but I still nearly squeezed Jake's hand to pieces as I went through the scene I had seen and overheard.

We went round the favourite son and second daughter bit a couple of times and they agreed with me that the gunmen had assumed they had Mum, Dad, John and myself in the cottage, and had bound and gagged the others as they only wanted to talk to Dad. Knowing the way Dad's mind worked, they then analysed what his reaction would have been to someone threatening to destroy his life's work.

It went back and forth for a while and they came to the conclusion that Dad would have worked out that there was still a route open to the caches through me, and that he had also worked out that he was not going to come out of the whole thing alive whatever he did, so they reckoned that Dad threw himself at the gunman in the hope that he might save the rest of his family. Unfortunately Dad hadn't reckoned on the gunman being *a completely ruthless bastard* – my words, not theirs.

'A hideous waste of a great mind, Miss Fenwick, I am truly truly sorry that you should have had to experience anything like that. However, what confuses me still is why you ran away rather than seeking help or waiting for the emergency services to arrive?'

I admitted that in retrospect it was probably not the cleverest decision of my life, but at that particular point in time I was convinced that if people knew I was still alive, then the gunmen would come back and kill me. Perhaps I had seen too much TV, but all I wanted just then was to find someone I could trust and the only people I trusted were Jake and his parents.

'Who is to know how any of us would have reacted in those circumstances,' said Edward, 'and it was just before they left the cottage that you heard the black man talk about *the Sheikh*? You are positive those are the words he used?'

I told him that was exactly what I heard – *that will keep the Sheikh happy.* There was lot of muttering and discussion amongst them and I asked if we could have a quick comfort break. I grabbed Jake and marched off out of the room. I wanted to pee, but I also wanted to ask Jake how he thought it was all going. He reckoned I was doing fine, and that there was lots of stuff going on in the background that we were not being told about and probably never would be. He gave me a quick hug and I nipped off to the loo.

When we got back, the mood in the library looked very serious.

'I am sorry we can't tell you more, but everything you have told us so far helps us put together a rather complicated jigsaw. Unfortunately we are still missing a few pieces, but that is our problem not yours. The next problem is that of the caches and I hope the not inconsiderable brain-power assembled here can help us understand what your father was up to.'

He walked to the door and called Terry and Christine in, who had been waiting patiently outside.

'Come in, you two, as the retrieval of these caches will no doubt involve some tramping round the countryside and I am not letting these two youngsters out there without your protection.'

Edward then asked us to divulge what we had managed to solve so far, so Jake and I took them through our reasoning. Having had to explain it all once to Uncle Bill, it was much easier the second time round. *grunt_futtock* made them smile, *F in cod* made them groan (Dad obviously didn't tell his worst jokes at committee meetings), the hobbies and attributes they agreed were undoubtedly a red herring, the clock puzzle and Phi were solved in about three seconds by Andrew, who shrugged and apologised that he had been a Maths professor in his previous career, and the diagonal was acknowledged as being a very logical result by a couple of the people present and had been confirmed by geochecker.

'So, Miss Fenwick and Mr Barton, if I may summarise so far?' asked Edward. 'We have two caches, both of which you have managed to solve and this geochecker thing has confirmed the solutions. However the coordinates are not actually correct as your father wanted to purposely mislead any searchers apart from yourself.' Jake and I reluctantly nodded our agreement with Edward's summary so far.

'You have gone through the conversation you had with your father, you have told us the content of the email, you have checked there is nothing hidden in the source of the webpage, and you say the only thing left are these hints *Fracture* and *Rocky*, which unfortunately do not ring any bells at this point in time?' Jake and I nodded again. 'Then I would suggest that first thing tomorrow morning the four of you, and Mutt of course, visit the two locations and see if anything comes to mind.'

We all agreed that made sense, even if it was incredibly frustrating, so he sent us off with Terry and Christine for some supper.

'I am sure your father has chosen a spot that will have some significance to you, and when you are *on the ground* so to speak, then something may well occur to you. We will all meet here again tomorrow evening to discuss progress. Terry, if you could take Miss Fenwick through the photographs we have assembled after supper, that would be most useful?'

Edward could see the determined expression on my face.

'Angela, we have assembled a range of photographs of assorted suspects for you to browse through in the hope that you may recognise one or more of the gunmen. I know you would probably like to leap out now and look for the caches, but firstly it is going to get dark very soon, and secondly I believe this is the highest priority at this point in time – OK?'

Well, I couldn't argue with that. Anything to catch those bastards was good with me.

Chapter 25

Hashim walked over to his brother's suite and knocked on the door. Hearing a somewhat exasperated *come in* he opened the door and found his brother hunched over the Professor's laptop almost pulling his hair out.

'Stay calm, Mansur, and tell me what you have discovered so far.'

'This is driving me mad,' Mansur said, 'I managed to find the details of the caches that the Professor hid for his children. There were two caches near where he lived, which have only been found by *TheMadProfessor*, and that was too much of coincidence for us to ignore.' Hashim nodded his agreement and his brother carried on.

'I solved the puzzles, which were easy, but that only gave me one half of the coordinates and I was getting nowhere. So as you suggested we had one of your American contacts, Hojo, approach this geocaching person called *Celo* and pretend to be the police.'

This had been one of Hashim's ideas. As there appeared to be a man, who checked all the entries and had access to the website, it seemed a logical idea to approach *Celo* and ask him to divulge the location of the two caches. Hojo had had no trouble in locating *Celo* and showed him a very convincing false id card. *Celo* had very helpfully given them the two locations, but in both cases they were simply in the middle of a field. Hojo and Chuck had visited both spots and could see nothing nearby, which made any sense at all. The logs on the caches from the other people who had solved the puzzle also showed that they couldn't find anything either.

'I have looked at the profile of the man setting the caches and it says rock climbing, scuba diving and freefall parachuting, but there is nothing of that kind anywhere near either of the locations and the only other help is these hints of *Fracture* and *Rocky*, two films which I have never seen, and the significance of which totally escapes me.'

Hashim wandered round the room pondering the problem. In a business situation, if he had a problem that was beyond his skills, he would simply employ the best expert in the field.

'Mansur, in your searches through this strange geocaching world, have you come across an expert, someone who seems to be better or quicker at solving these puzzles faster than anybody else?'

Mansur's eyes lit up, as he realised his brother had hit upon a solution that had escaped him as he had been far too involved in trying to solve the puzzles himself.

'Oh yes, there is a man who calls himself *Got2Bfirst*, and he seems to live for solving puzzles and finding them before anybody else.'

'Can you find his real name?'

'I have already got it,' grinned Mansur, 'I wrote emails, using an id I made up, to the cachers, who have failed to solve these two caches, pretending to be another cacher and they have all replied with their real names. They are a very open and friendly community. Let me just look him up – here you are, his name is David Hall and he works for a large insurance company as you can see from his email id.'

'Excellent, time for our American friend to get his police id out again and visit Mr Hall.'

The Sheikh marched back to his suite, picked up the phone and called Brutus. He quickly explained the situation and told him to get Hojo in contact with David Hall as fast as possible and report back.

'If he doesn't have the solution already, get Hojo to ask him to work on it as a top priority and let him know as soon as he has a breakthrough.'

A few hours later the phone rang in the Sheikh's suite and Brutus reported back that Mr Hall had been more than happy to try and help the police. 'Hojo told him he had been selected because he was without doubt the best puzzle solver in the neighbourhood, and the guy lapped it up. Unfortunately he doesn't have the answer yet, but he will let us know as soon as he has a breakthrough.'

The Sheikh returned to his brother's suite, pulled him away from the laptop and told him the news. Now for a very fine dinner with some of that excellent champagne they had in the Savoy cellar. He was never seen to be drinking a drop of alcohol in his home country, but this was London and it would be a terrible waste not to exploit the opportunity.

In fact, he would also ring that extremely efficient and discrete escort agency later and see what they could provide in the way of entertainment for Mansur and himself this evening. The blondes they had sent round last time had been absolutely stunning and worth every penny of the very considerable sum of money he had paid them. He and Mansur had always shared everything and the possibilities with four in a bed were always much more interesting.

Chapter 26

Unfortunately I didn't have any luck with the photos, which was a great shame so we piled off to bed to get some much needed sleep before the morning's search. I must admit it took me a long while to get off to sleep as my brain was still trying to solve the *Rocky* and *Fracture* clues. I must have fallen off eventually because I was fast asleep when there was knock on the door and Christine poked her head round the corner to tell me that breakfast would be ready in fifteen minutes.

I got showered and dressed in my new clothes – what a pleasure not to be in those manky old jeans. I wandered downstairs and found the others seated round the table tucking into a full English breakfast.

'I know this may not be the healthiest thing in the world,' said Terry, 'but I have no idea how long we are going to be out today, so I am recommending you follow one of our basic operational rules, which is to always stock up on food when you get the chance as you have no idea when the next meal is coming!'

He looked at us to make sure he had our attention.

'And now for the serious part. When we are outside this house, you are in our care and you will do exactly what we tell you. This is our job, and we know what we are doing, so leave that side of things to us - OK?'

Jake and I looked at one another and then back to Terry and Christine. We nodded like a couple of kids at school, and having seen the thugs with their guns, I personally was ecstatic to have an expert looking after me.

Half an hour later we had all piled into Terry's car and we set off for the nearest cache, which was actually the one in Headley. We parked in a little lane just off the road through Headley village and spotted the footpath leading away from the corner of the road. I had been through the village loads of times, but the path was definitely somewhere I had never even noticed before. Terry led the way, with Jake and me in the middle and Christine bringing up the rear, and we walked a few hundred yards down a fairly narrow path, after which it all suddenly opened out. A few seconds later and Terry's GPS said we were right next to the spot, which was in the field to our left. The others looked bewildered as they looked round at the nearby fence, a couple of trees and a signpost.

'Forget it, there's no cache here,' I told them as I jumped up and down with a big grin on my face, 'but I know what Dad meant by *Rocky* now!'

'Don't keep us in suspense, that's not fair. Come on,

I can't see any rocks round here, are we being stupid or what?'

They all looked at me expectantly, waiting for the answer, but I wanted to have a bit more fun before I revealed just how startlingly brilliant I was!

'Look around and tell me what you see in the field?' I asked.

'Grass?' I shook my head.

'Ponies?'

'Ta da, give that man a prize!' they still looked totally confused. 'Rocky was the name of my pony, when I was younger. So that's obviously what Dad meant by the clue. However, I must admit, he wasn't stabled up here, and I don't really know where to go next.'

We heard some people coming along the path, so Terry and Christine herded Jake and myself behind them, told us to talk to the ponies in the field behind us, and dropped their hands casually inside their pockets. Shit, I suddenly realised they probably had guns in there. A group of walkers came towards us and we moved to the side of the path to let them by but Terry and Christine ensured that they were always between us and the walkers.

Once all the walkers had gone, they both relaxed, and Jake started asking me questions about Rocky, and I explained that we used to ride him over to Headley, with Mum and Dad and John on the bikes and me on the pony, because there was a caravan up in the car park that served extremely good Cornish pasties, that Mum and Dad liked, and they had great chips too. As the caravan was not far away, we decided to drive up there and have a cup of tea and let Mutt have a good run round, but neither the tea, nor the fresh air did my brain any good and I stood there looking round the car park wondering if Dad had something hidden here.

'Penny for them,' said Jake with an enquiring look as he whistled for Mutt to come back.

'I don't think Dad would hide anything here as it is all rather open and exposed and Dad liked to place his caches in places that aren't so full of Muggles.'

'Muggles?'

'Oh sorry, that's what geocachers call people from the non-geocaching world. Come on, let's go check out the other one as Dad said we should do this one second and perhaps there is a clue down there that will help me up here.'

We drove down Pebble Hill, turned left at the bottom by the garden centre that Dad had used for the dummy coordinates, and went along till we found Rectory Lane on the left. We drove up to the end, passing over the railway line on the way, but the lane was narrow with no parking spots so we turned round and parked further down where a couple of footpaths branched off each way. It was all very depressing as I didn't recognise anything, and to be honest if geochecker hadn't shown *success* I would have been convinced that we were in the wrong spot.

I hooked my arm into Jake's, and pretended all was well, but I'm not sure he was convinced as we marched up the lane past Kemp's Farm and into the middle of a large field. And that's all there was at the location – a large field with nothing in it except for a few piles of cow shit. Shit was the right word.

Terry was playing with the GPS and looking around. 'Your Dad gave you diagonal as the clue, so let's try going diagonally. That corner up there looks promising.'

None of us could think of anything better so we marched to the north west corner of the field where there was a pretty little path going off to the left, which Terry told us was part of the Pilgrim's Way going across to Canterbury. The next bit along Reigate Hill was called the North Downs Way, and I told them that we had done bits of that up the top of the hill, but we had never been down here.

There was a tree on the corner that cried out to be a geocaching hide as it had a great big hole in the middle of its base, but we couldn't find anything and I couldn't see why Dad would expect me to come here. So Terry checked out the GPS again and said the diagonal went through the woods further up the hill, so we might as well check that and see if any of it intersected with our walks on the North Downs Way. I opened the little gate and we set off with Mutt racing up the hill on the scent of a rabbit or something.

A short while later we were at the edge of the woods. Terry said the GPS pointed left, so he started scouting around, but it didn't look promising. Mutt was still sniffing along on the trail of someone or something so I followed him up the hill cursing Dad under my breath for making it all too bloody difficult. On the other hand he had told me that he didn't want anyone else finding it. Right. Didn't say anything else about me not finding it!

I turned round to check where Jake and Terry were and nearly fell over with shock. I did know this path! I turned round on the spot. Looking upwards I recognised nothing but looking down I realised I had been here before, we had just come from above not below. Doh!

'Jake, Terry, come here, I know where we are! We rode our bikes down here. I just didn't recognise it from the other direction, but I've definitely been here before.' I was almost wetting myself with excitement, and Mutt was bouncing round wondering what all the fuss was about.

'Brilliant,' Jake came and gave me a big hug, 'now we just need to work out what *Fracture* means – any ideas?'

I cast my mind back to that bike ride.

'John was still fairly young, and Dad had told him to be careful going downhill, but he wasn't really listening as he was too excited about his new bike and yes....' I wandered up and down the path getting my bearings, 'he came down here too fast and crashed.'

The faces around me were all alight with excitement as we appeared to be homing in on the answer.

'Did he break any bones?' asked Christine.

'No, he didn't, but .., hang on a minute... yes, yes, he broke his watch-face and he was really angry as he had only just got it as a present from granny. Hang on a minute, let me do a quick reconstruction.'

I walked back up the path.

'I was up here, and John was flying down the path too fast, and then there was a crash and he shouted "blast" as that was his new swear word, that he had just learnt. Dad came rushing down to check he hadn't hurt himself and John was stamping his foot and saying blast, blast, blast. Dad told him that was probably a very good word to use as he appeared to have crashed into a blasted oak, and he made a big joke of a blasted crash blasting him into a blasted oak! John had no idea what a blasted oak was, but it made him laugh and Dad promised to buy him a new face for the watch. So folks, down here on the left we should find an oak what's been blasted!'

And there it was. Not as big as I remembered it, but I think bits must have fallen off over the years and that was my excuse for not recognising the spot straight away. Mutt started sniffing round the bottom of the tree and all four of us started searching in all its nooks and crannies. Hey presto, stuck away in the back of a hole in the middle of the trunk I could feel something. I carefully pulled my hand out and there it was, a little 35mm film canister, which was one of Dad's favourite cache containers.

'Got it, I've bloody got it, yeehah, whoopy do and all that sort of stuff.' There were high fives with Jake and he gave me a huge cuddle and a kiss that I must admit I made last rather longer than he had probably first planned, but hell I was dead chuffed and let's face it, Jake really is the dog's bollocks, so a girl has to take her chances, right? Anyway, I didn't detect any complaints from Jake, and I think we only stopped because there was a gentle cough from Terry and Christine, who were watching the path in both directions and wanted to see what was in the cache. Whoops, I had forgotten they were there, what a brazen hussy I am.

I cautiously removed the lid of the container and found a folded piece of paper inside, which said

Congratulations on finding the About Time cache.

I was a bit worried when I saw that we weren't the first people to find it, as the log had been signed, but then I realised it was signed by *TheMadProfessor* on the 1st April – Dad, and I started blubbing again. Jake took the cache from my hand and handed it to Christine, who walked away a few yards and dragged Terry with her so that I could try and compose myself in peace. I rested my head on Jake's chest and just sobbed and sobbed.

'It's not fair that those bastards should take my Dad away.'

Jake stroked my hair and told me I was spot on, and after a couple of minutes he suggested we looked at the cache to see how we could solve the next part and stuff it up the arses of the sodding gunmen. Poetically put, I thought, and called Terry and Christine back.

'Anything else on the piece of paper or in the cache?' we asked and Terry handed it to me saying there appeared to some German on there and some strange letters across the bottom. I showed Jake what was written on there

Wo ist es?
Q?Q? SSBC/AMDUGM

We all looked at one another hoping for some inspiration. *Wo ist es* was easy as that was German for *Where is it*, but the string of letters meant nothing to us at this point. We couldn't make any sense of it at all, so Jake changed the subject and asked me if anything down here had given me any inspiration for the *Rocky* clue.

'Good question. This one was obviously designed round an incident with John, so I would guess we are looking for a spot on a path up in Headley where Rocky or I did something stupid.'

Jake asked me whether I had ever fallen off Rocky, and I told him not be that cheeky, as I wasn't that bad a rider. I thought about it for a while and asked Terry to show me on the map where the diagonal line went through from here to the other cache. The first part went through something called Dawcombe Wood, where we had never been and across a couple of roads, so I rejected all that. The next section seemed to go through someone's house, a field and then it came to the interesting bit, which was up near the car park at Headley, where we had our cup of tea.

'We used to come out here after riding across from Walton, where Rocky had his field. Sorry to be tedious, but can we go back to Headley and walk back along the path I used to ride and see if we find anything?'

Terry thought it was a great idea as he had been dying to try one of the Cornish pasties I had spoken about earlier, so I stuck the cache and the precious piece of paper in my pocket as there was no way I was leaving that for anyone else and we marched back down the hill to the car in a semi-triumphant mood. One down, Dad and one to go – you'd be proud of me.

I am glad to say that the Cornish pasties and the chips were brill. I was slightly worried that this caching lark seemed to involve eating all the time, but at least we were walking it all off afterwards!

Suitably fortified we set off down the path that I used to ride with Rocky. I took the wrong turn a couple of times, which I couldn't quite explain until I realised that Rocky normally did the navigation. I pretended he was under my control, but he wasn't really. He knew the way home much better than I did, as he knew there was food when he got back to his field, but I told them I was on the right path now, and Terry confirmed that we were actually going almost parallel to the diagonal line.

'It's a funny old path this one, with quite high banks on each side as you can see, and Rocky was never totally happy coming down here and there is one spot where I always struggled to get him to go past as it seemed to spook him,' I was prattling on as we walked, and Jake stopped in his tracks.

'Angela, did you listen to what you just said?'

'Oh my God, the spot where he got spooked... it couldn't be could it?' and I started running down the path.

Terry grabbed me and told me go steadily, as he didn't want me out of his sight, and to just tell him when we were getting close. I calmed down and told him it was a couple of minutes down here on the left-hand side, where there should be the wreck of an old car on the side, which Rocky had hated.

My memory was improving, because just a short while later the rusty old wreck was sitting there and if that didn't cry out for a cache to be hidden inside it somewhere, then I was an idiot. I warned them that the cache was probably attached with a magnet as Dad had recently bought some lovely little magnets, that were super-powerful and which we all loved playing with. Only problem was that the wreck had all sorts of hidey holes in it, where you could hide a hundred caches if you tried hard enough, so Terry allocated us a portion each, whilst he kept watch. This time Jake came up trumps as he told us he had his arm right up inside the double skin of a wing and could feel something hidden away round the back.

'Bugger me, your Dad didn't want that found too quickly did he?' he commented as he withdrew his arm and proudly displayed another little 35mm film container. We opened it to find a similar piece of paper to last time with the expected *Congratulations on finding the no F in Greece cache* and the FTF signed by *TheMadProfessor*, but I was OK this time as I knew it was coming. What I was more intrigued by was what we what we would find at the bottom if anything, and the answer was this.

DA!
Q?Q? GMDUBC/AMSS

'Well DA is German for there, so that follows on from the last one – where is it, answer there, but where the hell is there? Oh Dad, are you listening up there, why couldn't you make it a bit simpler?'

'Put it in your pocket and pretend to play with Mutt,' Terry hissed at us, 'now!'

I thought he was being a bit bolshy, but then I heard people coming and I realised he was simply doing his job right and we pretended to fuss over Mutt as two Mums came past with their children on ponies and a dog wandering along behind. Mutt and he had a good sniff at one another and we all nodded hello, but again Terry and Christine positioned themselves between us and them as they were taking no chances.

We checked that there was nothing else hidden anywhere, and checked one another's nooks and crannies, if you see what I mean, finding absolutely nothing except rust, so we voted to go back to the safe house and study the two pieces of paper in peace and quiet to see if we could come up with anything.

Checking Jake's nooks and crannies was definitely high on my list. Hope he's thinking the same way? Hey, I'd solved two caches, so I deserved some reward didn't I?

Chapter 27

We were gathered again in the library, including Terry and Christine this time. Edward had an even worse combination of shirt and tie on and I wondered whether he got dressed in the dark. I suddenly realised he had started talking whilst I was checking out his total lack of dress sense.

'...which is why we have invited another couple of guests to come and help us, and you'll meet them in a minute.' Edward paused for a moment as he gathered his thoughts. 'The gentlemen in this room as you have probably guessed work in a profession, where we trust very few people. Therefore we have also decided that no-one outside this room should know that you are still alive if we can possibly avoid it, so I am not going to explain to our guests who you are. Continuing our rather elaborate but basically simple wordplay, I will simply call you Fern and George, if you have no objections?...Good. Terry, could you also ask our other guests to join us now please?'

Terry left the room and came back a couple of minutes later followed by two men, one of whom was limping slightly and both of whom looked slightly confused by the whole thing.

'Come in, come in,' said Edward. 'Mr Wilson and Mr Hall I believe? Do come in and sit down. Sorry to drag you away from whatever you had planned this evening, but I hope they explained this is truly a matter of national importance?' He looked at Terry, 'and can you please ask them to whistle up some tea and coffee and some of those rather good chocolate biscuits they have down here?'

Curiouser and curiouser I thought, so I whispered *who's that* to Jake and he just shrugged his shoulders as he was just as bewildered as I was. Mr Wilson was looking at Mr Hall as if he ought to know him, but his thoughts were interrupted by Edward as he took the middle of the floor again and looked at them both.

'Mr Wilson, I am sorry to start off the proceedings in a rather formal way, but I have to warn you that anything you see or hear in this room is subject to the Official Secrets Act, and I need you to acknowledge that fact before we continue.'

'Of course,' said a slightly startled looking Mr Wilson, 'a little surprising, but not totally unexpected after what you just said about national importance.'

'Thank you,' said Edward as he turned to Mr Hall, 'and you Mr Hall have been covered by the Act for quite some time.' Mr Hall confirmed that to be the case, even though he was no longer on active duty.

Edward turned back to Mr Wilson. 'Now, you are, I believe Sir, the person referred to as *Celo* by the geocaching community and your job is to approve cache placements?'

Ah, Jake and I could both see where this was going now, and Mr Hall suddenly looked a whole lot more interested as he leant over and shook Mr Wilson's hand.

'Yes, that is correct. *Celo*, as you no doubt know is Latin for hide, so it seemed an apt name.'

Well, you learn something every day I thought as Edward turned to Mr Hall and spoke to him, 'And you Mr Hall are known as *Got2Bfirst* in that community, due to your desire to be the first to solve and find puzzles?'

Mr Hall looked a bit sheepish, but admitted that was his particular raison d'être in the geocaching world.

'You are familiar with a cacher who called himself *TheMadProfessor*? And are you aware of his real identity?'

'Yes,' started Mr Wilson, 'as I've already explained to your American colleague yesterday, I have corresponded many times over the years with Professor Harold Fenwick, who called himself *TheMadProfessor* in the geocaching world.'

Edward looked startled by this. 'Sorry, I am confused – you said you have already explained this to our American colleague?'

'Yes, I assumed this request was a follow-up to that meeting. Don't you people talk to each other? I thought that was just something made up in books and films?'

Celo's smile began to slip from his face as he looked round the room and saw a series of extremely serious people shaking their head in turn to Edward's raised eyebrow of interrogation.

'Mr Wilson, I can assure that all the relevant parties are represented in this room, including our friends from across the pond, and I can categorically state that no-one from our side has been instructed to contact you before his afternoon, when we arranged for you to be invited here. When did this person approach you and what happened?'

Celo was now looking very uncomfortable, and explained that he had been contacted at work by a man claiming to be a member of the Surrey Police, and the id he had shown him claimed the same thing. *Celo* had been surprised by the American accent, but the man explained that he had been living here for years and accents were the one thing that took ages to disappear, and it was quite helpful in the summer as they dealt with a lot of American tourists.

The colour had drained from *Got2Bfirst*'s face as he raised his hand.

'Gentlemen, I fear the problem goes deeper than that. Can I take it that you also didn't arrange for anyone to contact me before this evening?' Shaking heads all round and worried expressions confirmed that he was right. 'Well, I had a visit from what sounds like exactly the same person this morning and I had also simply assumed this was an extension of that discussion.'

'Fern?' Edward looked across at me. 'Could you

please give us a quick description of the Americans you observed?

I was getting the hang of Edward slowly, and I was coming to the conclusion that he was a man, who played his cards close to his chest and didn't like to divulge anything until he had to. Jake gently squeezed my hand in encouragement and I described the large black guy, which got no reaction from *Celo* or *Got2Bfirst*, so I moved on to the second one, who was tall, thin and nerdy looking with brown hair, a rather sad little goatee, and I suddenly remembered he was left-handed. Don't know why I hadn't said that before, but I could now picture him in the cottage holding his gun in his left hand.

'Well that certainly sound like the chap I met,' said *Celo*, 'who does he work for then?'

Got2Bfirst also confirmed that he had met what sounded like the same person.

Edward looked at *Celo* and *Got2Bfirst* and reminded them that NOTHING went out of this room.

'I assume you have both seen the media coverage of the tragic death of Professor Fenwick?' They both nodded their heads in agreement. 'Please do not ask me to divulge my sources, but I am very sorry to inform you that the man you met was not only not a member of the Surrey Police, but was also one of the people responsible for the death of the Professor and his family.'

To say that *Celo* and *Got2Bfirst* looked shocked was an understatement, but *Celo* bounced back rapidly.

'Well that explains some strange emails I had from

Harold before he died.' Edward encouraged him to continue. 'Harold wrote to me a while ago asking what would happen if I were approached by the police and asked to divulge the location of a cache on our website to *assist them in their enquiries*, and I told him that I would obviously be duty bound to reveal it. He wrote back saying that was exactly what he had expected and was very commendable. This American chap came to me asking for the location of two caches placed by a new cacher called *grunt_futtock*, which he claimed was a pseudonym for the Professor.'

'Thank you, Mr Wilson, that completes another piece of the jigsaw. We believe Harold realised that some untrustworthy characters might try to convince you that they were policemen and get you to divulge information.'

Celo was looking more and more uncomfortable, and one of Edward's colleagues came forwards and whispered in Edward's ear. Edward nodded and looked across at *Celo*.

'Mr Wilson, my colleague thinks that you are now asking yourself not only what have you got yourself into, but also who are these people and whether they really are *the good guys*?'

Celo looked even more uncomfortable and gently nodded his head. 'Will you excuse me for a few minutes while I make a phone call, which I believe will set your mind at rest? Do help yourselves to those excellent biscuits and there are loos outside on the right if you need them.'

I grabbed Jake and hissed, 'Come with me,' and

pretended we were going to the loo.

When we got outside we turned a couple of corners and then I whispered in his ear, 'You know, he's not the only one who is beginning to think this is all a bit strange. No-one has shown us any identity and how do we know they aren't just trying to get at Dad's cache through me?'

Jake looked at me and shrugged. 'Surely, they must be the goodies. They came after we phoned the police, right?' He could see he hadn't convinced me. 'Look, see what comes up with this phone call, and if we're not happy we'll ask for proof before we carry on - OK?'

A couple of minutes later we were all back in the library waiting for Edward to finish his call. He was obviously waiting for someone on the phone and he mouthed *sorry, any minute now*. At last he smiled and said, 'Just putting you on the speaker-phone Colonel,' and a voice none of us recognised came across the room.

'Captain Hall, I hope your leg is not giving you too much trouble? Can you and Terry please confirm that you recognise my voice?'

Mr Hall sat up straighter in his chair and almost snapped off a salute. 'Yes, sir, absolutely.' Terry looked across at Mr Hall with an expression of respect. OK, this begins to make sense, member of the SAS and ex-member would be my guess.

'Miss Fenwick, can I first please pass on my condolences to you in this time of tragic loss? Your father will be missed by all of those, who worked with him, he was a fine man. I was occasionally a guest at those committee meetings and it was a pleasure to work with your father.' The voice paused. 'Ladies and gentlemen, I command an establishment, which is very well known to all of you, and I can personally vouch for all the gentlemen assembled in the room with you. The gentlemen you are with are working with have direct authority from the Prime Minister himself, with whom I have just been meeting and I have asked him to confirm that to all of you in a moment. Thank you and good luck.'

There was a slight pause and then a voice we all knew came down the phone.

'Miss Fenwick, I know your father was not my greatest fan, but his work has proved vital to the country on several occasions and he will be sorely missed. Can I please extend my deepest sympathies to you at this time, and assure you that Edward and his colleagues will do everything in their power to bring these dreadful people to justice. My apologies that is so short, but I have to get back into a meeting now. I hope we can meet when this is all over. Goodbye and good luck.'

Edward turned the phone off and turned to us, 'I won't embarrass *Captain* Hall by asking him to tell you any of his background. Suffice it to say that the Colonel told me he has proved his loyalty to this country on numerous occasions, and that he would still be on active duty if he hadn't suffered a very unfortunate injury when protecting a VIP, due I believe to the VIP not following your instructions?' Mr

Hall nodded sheepishly.

'So I hope that all of that has put your mind at rest Mr Wilson, and I am afraid you and Mr Hall have just learnt another piece of information, WHICH DOES NOT LEAVE THIS ROOM, namely that the brave young lady sitting over there is, in fact, the daughter of the late Professor Fenwick. I am sorry, Miss Fenwick, but the Colonel and the PM said they couldn't possibly talk to you without passing on their condolences as they thought that would be callous in the extreme.'

Edward then spent a minute or two explaining to *Celo* and *Got2Bfirst* that I had survived the attack on my family by sheer luck and had been able to observe the men responsible. After we had talked about the caches, he was going to ask all of us to study their extensive files of photographs to see if we could identify the villains. I had had no luck last night, but they had brought a whole bunch of new ones along from their American contacts and they hoped that might help us identify the gunmen. It was fascinating to watch *Celo* and *Got2Bfirst* as their faces went from shock, through sympathy to anger, and finally to dogged determination.

Chapter 28

To say the atmosphere was electric in the library would have been an understatement. Jake smiled at me and said *told you so*, and I could see Terry looking at Captain Hall in a new light. I felt as if a weight had been lifted off my shoulders as large parts of my paranoia began to dissolve and *Celo* and *Got2Bfirst* were chomping at the bit to find out more.

'Right,' said Edward, 'now we can turn our attention back to the caches?' There were nods of eager anticipation from all round the room. 'Mr Wilson, can you please tell us exactly what the American impostor told you and what he wanted to know?'

Celo explained that the American had claimed that he was a policeman working on the Professor Fenwick case, and that the police had cause to believe that the Professor had left some vital information hidden in one of his recent caches. The police believed that the caches were placed under a pseudonym of *grunt_futtock*, because they were two recent caches that had only been found by *TheMadProfessor* and nobody else, and the American has asked *Celo* to confirm that the two ids did in fact belong to the Professor.

Celo had been able to confirm the first one as he had been corresponding with the Professor for years, but the second one was new to him and all he had was the profile on the website, which said he/she was an adventurer from Surrey, whose hobbies were rock climbing, scuba diving and freefall parachuting, and the email id of *grunt_futtock* on hotmail didn't help either.

'That doesn't sound like your father, does it Angela?' said Edward, who had dispensed with the Fern and George malarkey now that the cat had been let out of the bag, 'so I assume that is confirmation of the trick you told us about to hide the caches under a different name and give that person some weird hobbies, which didn't match your father's at all and wouldn't help anyone solve the puzzles?'

Got2Bfirst nodded his head in acknowledgement of a neat trick.

'Not quite in the spirit of the geocaching rules, but perfectly understandable in the circumstances, and that explains why I have spent hours researching all the wrong websites!'

Celo then went on to tell us that the American had asked him to look up the solutions to the two caches. There was one called *About Time* and one called *There's no F in Greece*.

'And you obviously gave the locations to the American impostor as you thought you were helping the police?' and *Celo* looked very embarrassed as he confirmed that he done exactly that yesterday.

'Do not blame yourself, sir, you thought you were assisting the police, which was most laudable, and the good news is that Professor Fenwick set the whole thing up so that the coordinates on the geocaching website aren't the right answers, so no harm done.'

Celo looked very upset, and explained that the whole point of geocaching was that the caches should be locatable from the information published on the website. Edward said that whilst that was to be applauded for a hobby, this was a seriously different proposition, and he asked me to explain just what my father had been trying to do and how far we had come so far in unravelling his trail of clues.

So I started with Dad telling me how he wanted to set up a set of caches for John and me to do when we came back from the Lake District, which would lead to the final cache with the USB stick in it. Fortunately I had got the hang of Edward's distrust by now didn't reveal what was on the USB stick.

I carried on explaining that because Dad didn't want anyone else to find the caches and the final prize, he had spent some time conjuring up a scheme whereby he could publish the caches in such a way that *Celo* would accept them, but no-one would be able to solve them except my brother and I. *Celo* looked even more upset, and I told him that Dad was fully intending to update the caches as soon as I had found them so that other people could find them too, but that the contents of the USB stick were so important that he had to protect them with all sorts of tricks and puzzles that no-one would solve.

'In fact, Angela, I think it is now time to reveal the next step in the story – could you take us through today's adventures please?'

So I ran through the day's adventures, but I didn't want to bore them with how stupid I had been at the beginning, so I started with the cache at the bottom of the hill and John falling off his bike, moved on to the pony field giving me Rocky and ending up with the car wreck. Sounded very easy when you summarised it, but at least *Got2Bfirst* admitted that he would never have been able to crack them based on the information my father had given on the cache pages. I then showed them the two caches and the two pieces of paper, giving us:

Wo ist es?
Q?Q? SSBC/AMDUGM
DA!
Q?Q? GMDUBC/AMSS

Which left most people totally baffled, but had *Got2Bfirst* absolutely hooked. The conversation went round and round, but *Got2Bfirst* said that he had actually worked best in a small group, and would really just like to sit down with Jake and me to hammer this thing out. He also pointed out that he was happy to work on it till all hours of the morning as that was embarrassingly normal and being single there was no-one, who was going to worry about him being out late..

'Admirable, but as I said before I am afraid we have a higher priority first. Namely, before you start taxing your brains with Professor Fenwick's latest puzzle, I would like you to study the photographs that have been brought in today and see if you can identify the impostor who visited you?'

Which was fine by me as I had been thinking about the puzzle for hours and got nowhere.

'Well, in that case, I suggest that you all adjourn to the study next door where the photos have been put out ready for you, and when you have finished with those there is a PC with broadband connection and a wireless network for Jake's laptop awaiting your efforts – I have given Terry details of the passwords. For the moment my colleagues and I will remain here and make some telephone calls. My apologies if I repeat that nothing you two have learnt in this room leaves this room, and I'm afraid Mr Wilson that includes talking to your wife and family! Awkward, I know, but if you could just tell them that you were helping the police with an investigation, that would be marvellous? Many thanks.'

After they had all left the room, DCI Jenkins walked through from the room next door where he had been listening to the conversation.

'Well, Detective Chief Inspector, I would say Miss Fenwick is beginning to look more and more in the clear?' was Edward's comment as he saw him come in.

'Yes, she is certainly telling a good story, but I would still like to talk to her. I hardly need to remind you that she tells us the invention was worth billions, and that's an enormous incentive. Until she manages to produce one of these alleged gunmen, she will continue to be a suspect in my eyes.'

'Well, if she is lying, she is worthy of at least ten Oscars, but we have both seen some magnificent liars in our time, and you have your job to do Detective Chief Inspector, so I suggest you interview her first thing tomorrow morning. All right?'

Chapter 29

We hurried through to the study, in my case because I wanted to find the bastards who had killed my family, but I think in *Got2Bfirst*'s case it was because he was dying to get at the final puzzle. On the table were three folders of photographs, and Terry allocated us one each, telling us to take our time and swap the folders over when we were done. Jake couldn't really help at this stage, so he sat in the corner quietly firing up his laptop and playing with Mutt. I found nothing in the first one and neither did the others, so we swapped them round and half way through the second I screamed out that I had got one of them.

'There, that big black bastard, that's the one ....' Jake rushed across and grabbed me as I started to rage.

Celo and *Got2Bfirst* looked somewhat shocked by my outburst, but they hadn't been there and seen what this shit had done. Terry asked us to carry on checking the remaining photos whilst he went next door to report success.

'Sorry to interrupt, Sir, but Angela has found one of them, a Brutus Carmichael.'

Edward turned to his American colleague, Charles, who checked some files and nodded his head.

'Ouch, a VERY nasty piece of work. Brutus Carmichael, born in Detroit 18 July 1970, nickname *"The Brute"*. Ex Special Forces, nearly killed an officer, served time in gaol, left the military before we could chuck him out. Currently wanted for the murder of a young man, who appears to have done nothing wrong except make a rude hand gesture at him, and is being sought by the police – they will be very interested to hear he has turned up over here.' Charles winced and looked sick as he skip-read some more details. 'Mm, appears to be one of those unfortunate examples of where we train someone to kill, but they can't control themselves. All I can say is that you want to watch out if you come up against him Terry; her poor father really had no chance against a man like that.'

Edward came through and congratulated me on my success and promised me he would talk to me about him later, but for the moment the important thing was to see if we could identify anybody else. The bad news was that an hour later we had exhausted the files and none of us could find a trace of the American impostor, and I couldn't find the two I had seen at the cottage. At least I had got one of the bastards though.

At that point *Celo* took his leave explaining that he was only good at checking caches and was absolute rubbish at solving them, so he would leave us in the capable hands of *Got2Bfirst*. The rest of us clustered round the table with the PC and started looking at Dad's strange puzzle again:

Wo ist es?
Q?Q? SSBC/AMDUGM
DA!
Q?Q? GMDUBC/AMSS

'Right, my name is David by the way,' said *Got2Bfirst* and we all shook hands and introduced ourselves as we hadn't got round to that before. 'I'm very sorry about your family and friend, it sounds absolutely awful... but as I understand it, the best thing we can do apart from identifying the shits involved is to find these caches your father left behind?'

As Jake and I nodded our agreement, he continued, 'You obviously know the basics of caching or you wouldn't have found these. I apologise if I state anything obvious, but let me run through what I've thought of so far.'

'Assume we have got nowhere!'

'OK, round here the coordinates all tend to be North 51 something and West 00 something, so most of us don't even bother to set puzzles for those parts of the coordinates, and that was your father's usual style as well. So that leaves us with two strings of letters, one of which I assume is North and the other West, for the moment we'll assume the first one is North and the second West.'

We agreed that that made sense so far.

'That gives us a string of twelve letters in each case plus a couple of question marks, which is a bit unusual as we actually only need five digits from each to complete the coordinates. Now it could be fourteen characters including the question marks, divided by two gives seven numbers, but as I said before one string would start 51 and the other 00 and they both start with Q?Q?' David paused for thought, 'so I am guessing that the question marks are superfluous and maybe the QQ as well, and your father is trying to tell us that each pair of characters represents a number.'

Jake and I were happy with all that as we had come to a vaguely similar conclusion, but not nearly as quickly and easily.

'Now the next thing we have to get into our heads is that this is nothing to do with *grunt_futtock*, it is your father's mind we are trying to understand. Therefore I am going to reject anything he put in *grunt_futtock*'s profile as I believe all that information to be a red herring.'

'But Dad *could* speak German,' I pointed out.

'Yes, but I think that's another of your father's tricks,' David continued with a determined look in his eye. 'Just bear with me for a moment, because I've been thinking about this ever since I first saw the puzzle. If we assume this is German, then we just get where is it, answer there, and then a string of letters that you are supposed to think are German, and the Du looks suspicious as that is German for you, and SS might be well known in Germany, although best forgotten and I honestly don't think your father would go anywhere near that idea, but words beginning with Q and words beginning with C are relatively rare in German from memory.'

'True, I can't think of many. Quelle and Quatsch for Q and Chance for C, and I think the German for cache is Cache?'

'Yes, but Q would not be question in German would it?'

'Ah, see what you mean, no. Frage is the German for question.'

'So,' said David, who was really getting into this and enjoying himself, 'your father would be unlikely to write Q? for a question if he were writing German, so let's work on the theory that German is a red herring for the moment. If we look at your father's hobbies, which I know well from doing lots of his caches...yes, here they are in his profile...music, photography, nice walks with caches, Harry Potter. Let's go through them and see if anything works. Music, unlikely as the letters don't match any scale I can think of, and your father already used jazz scales in one of his caches, and sharps and flats in some others; photography looks dodgy as I can't see anything here with shutter speeds or apertures – again he did a whole series of caches with photography; walks with caches doesn't really trigger anything, which leaves Harry Potter as the best candidate for the moment.'

'Something to do with Quidditch?' suggested Jake and we looked up the members of a team, wondering if S was the Seeker, B the Beater and C the Chaser, but couldn't make any sense of the rest. We also couldn't work out what he meant with BC/AM – something divided by something else. Before Christ divided by the morning made no sense to any of us. We sat there staring at various combinations and getting nowhere.

'Ah, now why has he done that?' asked David thinking aloud. 'Yes, yes, that could be it – Jake look up Dumbledore's Army in Wikipedia. You see, your father has written DA, where I would have expected him to write Da and Du or du, if it were German. Why the capitals? I am thinking Harry Potter and DA in the books was Dumbledore's Army - your father once set a cache under the pseudonym of Professor Dumbledore, because it amused him and allowed him to set lots of Harry Potter questions for us all to answer. I had to go back and reread all the bloody books to do that one!'

Jake couldn't find a list of members of the Army on Wikipedia, but he showed us one he found on the Harry Potter Lexicon website. We tried all sorts of combinations using the people's names and the numbers used on the website, but nothing made any sense. For instance the only R in Dumbledore's Army was Ron Weasley, who was number 29 and that just didn't get us anywhere. Shame, we seemed to be going the right way, but David told us this was typical with puzzle caches, you would get a couple of things, get all excited and then it would all fall apart.

'Trust me, you will know when you have it, because it will all click into place. It's part art and part science reall...'

'Art, ' Jake interrupted, 'sorry David, you just said

Art and DA is also Dark Arts – how about that?'

We turned back to the PC and looked up Dark Arts in Wikipedia, and started reading about the curses, the Horcruxes and all sorts of other things, but the only thing we could find that matched was Severus Snape for SS.

'Well, he always wanted to be in charge of Defence Against the Dark Arts, but he didn't manage it did he?' said Jake as he clicked on various links, 'whoops, sorry, I forgot he got what he wanted in book six.'

David's eyes lit up, 'How about the other years, who were the teachers then?'

Jake clicked on the link for Defence Against the dark Arts and read us the list, 'Galatea Merrythought before it all started, Quirinus Quirrell in book 1, Gilderoy Lockhart in book 2, Remus Lupin in book 3 ... my favourite book... Barty Crouch disguised as Alastair Moody in book 4, Dolores Umbridge in book 5 ...hiss hiss... Severus Snape in book 6 and Amycus Carrow in book 7. How does that look?'

David had been scribbling down the names and now he had a piece of paper in front of him on which he had written

GM = 0, QQ = 1, GL = 2, RL = 3,
BC or AM = 4, DU = 5, SS = 6, AC = 7

'I simply wrote down the initials and years as you went along and BC/AM looks good doesn't it? How about the two strings now? I think we have to ignore the question marks as another red herring and call those QQ, so this is what we get...'

QQ SS BC/AM DU GM = 1 6 4 5 0

And

QQ GM DU BC/AM SS = 1 0 5 4 6

'...which means we end up with N 51° 16.450 W 000° 10.546 as the solution, which you could argue has a logical flow on from the diagonal ones, but with a bit of a twist – where's that?'

Jake tabbed over into Google Earth and entered the coordinates, which zoomed in on a person's house. He turned the screen to me and invited me to take a look as he thought I might recognise whereabouts it was. I wondered what he meant and then I looked. Did I recognise it? Of course, I recognised it, it was our house! Dad had led us all round the place to end up back at our own house.

David was looking bemused, so we explained to him that the solution was my house, and he reckoned that proved that he had solved the puzzle correctly as it was too much of a coincidence. Terry went to talk to Edward again and he came back to collect us and take us through to the library. I couldn't wait to get back home and see if Dad had left something for me.

Most of the others had left, so when we got to the library it was just Edward and Andrew. They both looked up as we walked in and Edward raised his eyebrows in interrogation.

'We've cracked it!' I announced triumphantly. 'Well, to be honest it was mainly David, sorry Mr Hall and Jake, but at least I recognised the final location, which believe it or not is our house!'

I couldn't understand why Edward's face fell at this point and I looked at him for an answer.

'Miss Fenwick, we were going to have tell you at some stage, and now unfortunately appears to be the time. I am very sorry to say that your house was burgled whilst you were away in the Lake District and the whole place was ransacked. They took all your father's equipment like PCs and other stuff, so I am very sorry to say that we may have missed the boat.'

Talk about being slapped in the face with a wet fish! I hadn't worked through the implications of what I had overheard in the cottage. Of course they had been down to our house and searched it. SHIT!

'However, there is of course no harm in taking a look tomorrow as your father may well have hidden something that like the caches is obvious to you and meaningless to anyone else, so Terry and Christine will take you there tomorrow. I have arranged for a team of specialists to give the house a thorough sweep for any nasty surprises, and then you can go over there in the afternoon – all right?' he paused to check I was OK with that.

'Good, because we have another guest here, whom you might recognise from the television, and he would like to chat to you tomorrow morning.' At that point DCI Jenkins got up from the armchair where he had been hiding and introduced himself, explaining that he would like to run through where they had got to so far with me in the morning and clear up a few loose ends.

Edward checked we were all paying attention, 'Now, Andrew and I have come up with rather a cunning plan, which we would like you all to listen to.'

Chapter 30

'When can I expect the funds to be transferred?' Brutus asked the CEO of one of the world's largest oil companies in nervous anticipation. As soon as he had got wind of this assignment from the Sheikh, he had seen the obvious possibilities of setting himself up very comfortably for the rest of his life. Copying the information before passing it on had been child's play. This was the pay-off he had always deserved, and he had already bought his estate and his yacht in his mind. The *A-rab* would never find him.

'Mr Carmichael, I don't really like repeating myself, but as an extremely large amount of my cash is involved I will make myself perfectly clear. The first part will be transferred to your account at the end of the Conference, provided no-one releases any details at that event. The rest will be transferred when I have secured a successful patent. So don't try selling it to anyone else, son, or I'll have your big black testicles for golf-balls – is that clear enough?'

Brutus hated being threatened, but for the amount of money that was involved he was prepared to eat shit. Lots and lots of it.

Chapter 31

The Well House used to be Dad's local when he was growing up. His favourite time had been when they had loads of snow and couldn't get the cars out of the drive of his parent's house, so they tobogganed to the pub down the lanes and across the fields. Proper beer they had in those days, he would always tell us, coming straight out of barrels behind the bar and none of this designer wind-water they had nowadays. The beer was still hand-pumped, which made Jake happy.

*

I'd spent a couple of hours with DCI Jenkins, and I think he was now convinced that I wasn't some vengeful daughter out to get her hands on her father's invention, but as he explained to me it was his job to suspect everybody. It appears that the burglars had pretended to be the local Water Company, and had parked their van in our drive whilst they looted the house. The lovely old couple opposite had spotted them, but thought they were bona fide, and I confirmed that I hadn't heard anything from Mum or Dad about the drains being up the twist in any way. DCI Jenkins had also contacted the Water Company and they had no record of anyone visiting our house, so I think he realised that unless I was in some conspiracy up to my neck, I couldn't have burgled the house whilst I was on the way up to Cheshire.

The post-mortem had also confirmed that my father had been shot, and there were traces of plastic from the cuffs on my mother's, brother's and Susan's wrists. That had me in tears again for quite a while and I spent a long time asking him if I could have saved them. He told me that there was no way I could have got into that cottage and there was also no way the fire brigade could have got there in time, which started to make me feel slightly less guilty. I asked how Susan's parents were taking it all, and he told me that they were obviously distraught, but they would help in any way they could to bring the gunmen to justice.

*

We were sitting at the table in the bay window, which gave us a good view of the path in from the car park without anyone being able to see us. Edward's plan was really quite simple. He had got David Hall aka *Got2Bfirst* to call the American impostor and say he had a lead on the caches. He was meeting a couple in the pub called *Haensel and Gretel* who had found one of them by chance but were struggling with the clue they had found, so had offered to join forces, and would the American *policeman* like to join him when he met up with them. The impostor had, of course, been unable to resist. My job was to see if he was the same person as I had seen in the cottage and then to quietly disappear whilst Terry and Mr Hall did their stuff.

Jake and I were trying to act calm and nonchalant, which is why poor Mutt was getting stroked to death. Christine and DCI Jenkins were doing her best to make small talk, and Terry was sitting by himself in the garden waiting for my confirmation. I thought I was ready for all this, but when I saw the tall gunman walk over to David's car all I could do was grab Jake's hand and nod – speech was impossible. Christine whispered *positive visual* into her little mouthpiece thing and Terry's glance wandered nonchalantly round the garden checking everyone and everything.

David and Hojo entered the pub and looked for a couple matching *Haensel and Gretel's* description with no luck, so they got a couple of drinks and sat at a table in the main bar. We had made up the name when we first started the cache search at Jake's house and we had spent last night filling in a profile and a few dummy logs on geocaching, in case the gunman looked them up. We pretended they were two 50-year-old ramblers, who were new to geocaching. A hint of truth, if not quite accurate.

After a few minutes the phone behind the bar rang,

and the barman called out for a *Got2Bfirst*? David wandered over and said that was his nickname and took the phone. This had all been prearranged of course, and the story was that *Haensel and Gretel's* car had unfortunately broken down and they would have to arrange another meeting at a later date.

Christine had positioned herself so that she could see the entrance door, so when David and the American got up to leave she could warn Terry, who picked up his half empty glass and started walking down towards the pub. I don't know what happened next as we couldn't see round the corner, but a few seconds later Terry and David came round the corner propping up the American between him and apologising to a couple coming the other way for their friend's inability to hold his drink. As they reached the car park two more men got out of a car and simply took the American off their hands and shoved him in the back of their car. Terry and David signalled to us to come and join them and the three of us calmly got up and left. I say calmly, but my legs were like jelly and Jake had to help me. DCI Jenkins definitely had a different look in his eye, now that he had another suspect to interview.

'One down, two to go,' Terry grinned. 'Knowing he was left-handed was key, well done Angela. David is going back to the safe house as arranged, and we'll go and check out your parents' place – OK?'

Chapter 32

The police had keys for the house as they had been round to the neighbours when we had been burgled, and somehow I didn't think it was the right time to tell them there was another set hidden in the garden. I must admit I was setting out on this particular part of the search with mixed feelings. One half of me was intrigued to see if I could find something the gunmen couldn't and the other half was worried about what state the house would be in.

As we drove in all I could see was that funny police tape all round the place to stop people going in. Christine had made me put a baseball cap and sunglasses on so that none of the neighbours would recognise me, and as a little extra touch she had got us all jackets to wear with POLICE written on them. Sitting in the drive was another car that I didn't recognise, but Terry told me that Edward had arranged for the experts to give the place another thorough check before we went in as the house had been left empty for a while and they wanted to ensure that the gunmen hadn't come back and left any nasty surprises.

A few minutes later a man came out of the house and approached our car, and handed over the keys.

'Our colleagues have been through the whole house with the dogs and couldn't find any trace of explosives. We've also swept the whole house for bugs and you're clear.' All of which was a bit frightening, but also reassuring.

Inside the house it didn't actually look too bad. Yes, there were gaps all round the place where PCs and stereos and other stuff were missing, but they had been surprisingly tidy. I had been expecting to find things lying all over the floor and to have graffiti plastered all over the walls, but thinking about it they had just been after Dad's work so there was no need to vandalise the place. Wandering around I could see Mum's PC had gone, Dad's lab was totally cleared out, but Dad had done a lot of that before we left, and in his study his two PCs were gone.

His piano was also lying in pieces on the floor and I walked round it very gingerly as I thought about the bomb that had been in there even though they had been through the whole house and declared it safe.

My bedroom looked pretty much as I had left it. Jake asked me if the gunmen had made all this mess, and I quietly explained that it wasn't messy, it was just my filing system, and believe it or not I could see that nothing had really been disturbed. It was all so frustrating. I couldn't see anything that stood out at all, and if there had been I am sure the gunmen would have found it.

Checking once more that it was safe, I asked if I could have a few moments alone in Mum and Dad's bedroom, as that was where the coordinates actually pointed. Terry checked it out, and then came back and quietly nodded, so I wandered through to say goodbye to Mum and Dad. The first thing I saw was Dad's dressing gown hanging up and I walked over to smell his aftershave. Then I sat down on the stool at Mum's dressing table looking through her things and just fell apart. I don't know how long I was sitting there crying, but the next thing I heard was a gentle knock on the door and Christine's head poked round.

'Thought you might like a cup of tea?'

I nodded my thanks and grabbed a big handful of tissues from Mum's box. Christine came over and knelt next to me and held my hand asking me if I was ok. She explained that Jake had wanted to come up, but she had told the chaps to stay downstairs, as this was probably a time for the *girls* to be together.

'Thanks, I think Jake must be fed up with me bursting into tears all the time.'

'Don't be silly – that boy would jump off a cliff for you if you asked him. We were talking about you downstairs and if he's not seriously smitten, then I'm amazed. I think you'll find that he just doesn't want to take advantage of you when you are so vulnerable.' Well, I didn't want him jumping off a cliff, but jumping into bed with me wouldn't be a bad start. Christine saw me cheer up and was casually looking round the bedroom, 'Your Dad liked reading then?' I nodded as she could see there were books on the windowsill, on the bedside cupboard and on the floor, 'and I see he likes the same sort of stuff as I do – he's got all the latest ones here from Dick Francis, Ken Follett, Kate Mosse, Clive Cussler...'

'He's got a new Clive Cussler? He didn't tell me about that one!'

I explained that I read almost all of Dad's books and he always told me about the new ones he had bought, but I hadn't seen the new Clive Cussler yet. Christine handed it over and I definitely hadn't seen it before. The strange thing was that Dad appeared to be half way through it as there was a bookmark in the middle, so why hadn't he taken it with him? I opened the book and saw that he was using an envelope as the bookmark, which was also strange as he almost always used an old boarding card from one of his flights. I turned the envelope over and let out a whoop of joy.

'Look, look what it says on the envelope,' I pointed excitedly, '*grunt_futtock*! It must be something to do with the caches.' Christine called out to the others to come and join us as I opened the envelope. I could hear feet running up the stairs and Mutt's smiling face and wagging tail appeared shortly before Jake and Terry.

'What have you found?'

'There's an envelope here stuck in a book that Dad would have passed over to me soon to read and it says *grunt_futtock* on it!' and I showed them the envelope.

'Go on then, what's inside.'

I prayed that this was really something useful, and I hadn't got them all excited over nothing...

Well done grunt_futtocks!
You have found the first two caches and they have led you here. Now for the final clue – What do you get if you throw a piano down a coal mine?

'Brilliant, that must be the next part,' said Jake with a big smile, 'your Dad had obviously planned to give you that when you solved the first two caches. Now what was the question again?'

'What do you get if you throw a piano down a coal mine?' they all looked at me blankly.

'Well the good news is that I know the answer as it's another of Dad's old jokes, but I don't know where it gets us.'

'And the answer is?'

'Whoops, sorry, the answer is *a flat miner*'

There was a groan and a small nod from Jake who said it was awful but quite clever musically. He explained to the rest of us that it was a pun on *A Flat Minor*, which was one of the keys that you play music in.

'Keys, did you just say keys?' I cut across Jake's explanation as a light-bulb began to glow in my brain.

'Yes, you must remember a bit of music from school? Music is written in different keys, and A flat ...'

' ... and the keys to this house are hidden in the garden – come on let's go and look. Damn, I was going to go and look there anyway, but those two chaps who were here earlier gave us the set from the neighbours so I forgot.'

So we all went back down to the family room and I was about to unlock the patio door and rush out, but Terry wouldn't allow it. He told us all to stay indoors whilst he did a quick recce of the garden. Mutt thought we were all going out to the garden to play a game and picked up an old tennis ball lying there. Terry started throwing the ball round the garden and it looked very casual, but I could see that he was slowly but surely getting to every corner. Mutt got very interested in one particular spot in the back hedge next to the garden shed, which I remembered as being one of our favourite hiding places when we were kids. Terry wandered over to see what he was looking at and continued his walk round the garden.

After a while he came back to the patio door, took me into the utility room and quietly asked me where the keys were hidden. I told him there was a nesting box attached to the cherry tree, and they were in there, all he had to do was unhook it. He told us to wait inside and wandered nonchalantly back round the garden playing with Mutt. As he passed the tree he knocked the nesting box off by mistake, said *shit I'll have to mend that*, and brought it back to the house.

'Knocked this off the bloody tree and broke it – I'll mend it and put it back. Come on Mutt.' Jake and I were looking at him in total confusion, but Christine just queried him with her eyes and he nodded. He took Jake and me into the utility room again.

'OK, listen carefully. There are no windows here, so no-one can point a microphone at us. It looks like someone has been watching us – Mutt found his hiding spot in the garden and I could smell chewing gum and cigarettes – none of your family smoked did they?' I shook my head. 'He's not there at the moment, but I assume he's nearby, so we will see if we can flush him out. Get the keys out of this thing and we'll bash a couple of nails and put it back.'

The box was a fake, and the hole at the front was actually taped over so that birds couldn't use it. I turned the box round and showed them that the back had a couple of little latches on it that you could undo. I took the back off, and inside there was a set of house keys with a beautiful little USB stick attached to them, which I stuck inside my bra – no-one was going there unless I agreed! I handed the box back to Jake who wandered through to the garage with me saying in a loud voice that we should find a hammer and nails in there somewhere. A few bangs later and the box was repaired. Terry called us all into the utility room and explained his plan.

'I've called up reinforcements. As soon as I hear they are in place I am going to put the box back and make it obvious that the USB stick was in there. That means whoever is out there will have to follow me if they want to get it back. Christine will stay here to protect you till she gets the all clear.' We all nodded and wished him luck. Who are these unsung heroes who risk their lives to help people like me? Terry opened the garage door and got a bag from the boot of the car and brought it in to the garage. He rearranged the contents slightly, handed Christine a little machine-gun thing and took out a funny looking jacket, which he laid out ready on the top of Mum's car. His mobile rang and he just nodded and said he was ready and would be going out of the drive and driving straight up the road opposite as that led to the quiet roads up by the heath.

With everything in place he went back out to the garden with the nesting box and hung it in the tree. As he walked back to the house, he said out loud 'well, who would have guessed that was a place to put keys – rather clever. Wonder what the USB stick has on it? I'll take it back to the station and let them look, whilst you finish off here.' At that point things moved fast. Terry stepped through the back room and marched into the garage where he flung on the jacket and grabbed the bag. Then he threw the bag in the car, and was moving down the driveway before we had even blinked. I had the garage door shut, Jake had the patio door locked and Christine had us herded into the utility room with her pistol and Terry's machine-gun out ready for anything.

Chapter 33

Chuck couldn't believe it. He'd thought he'd check the house out again as apparently the Professor might have left another USB stick lying around, but he hadn't expected anyone to be there. *Fungus face* was going to join him later after he had checked out another lead with the crazy cache guy. He was checking the back of the house again this morning when two police cars arrived. The first one had him worried when the dog came out, but they just went into the house and he assumed they were sniffing round for hiding places, which could be interesting. Then a second car had arrived with another two policemen, who took over when the first team left. Definitely searching for something.

So he had settled himself down in the undergrowth and made himself comfortable. He hadn't really been prepared for a long wait, so when he had to take a leak, he just rolled over slightly and did it against the bottom of the fence, which wasn't perfect but he wasn't planning on coming back here. On a proper surveillance operation he would have had plastic bags with him and taken any bodily excretions away with him, but he had been caught out this morning. All he had with him was some chewing gum to stave off his craving for a cigarette. Then another car arrived with two more policemen and two policewomen, and another darned dog.

He pointed his binoculars at the windows and tried to see what they were doing, but they were obviously at the front of the house because he only got the occasional glimpse of them. If only they had planted some bugs when they went in the first time, but they hadn't expected to come back. A parabolic microphone would be handy as well, and he made a mental note to tell *fungus face* to add one to their regular kit for future jobs. He tried to call *fungus face*, but couldn't get any response, which probably meant that he was in a bad network coverage location.

Suddenly there was movement in the kitchen – typical, making a cup of tea. What was it with the Brits and their tea? He'd murder for a Starbucks right now. A couple of minutes later they all disappeared again and then they all appeared in the back room with the dog. Shit, it looked like they were coming outside, which meant he needed to be elsewhere. He had, of course, got his escape route planned, so he gathered his minimal equipment, checked he hadn't left any litter behind and backed away further into the undergrowth, where the dog shouldn't come sniffing round.

A short while later one of the policemen came out and started playing ball with the dog. They got very close to where he had been hiding up and he thanked the Lord that he had moved away. A couple of minutes later the dork knocked the bird thing off the tree and took it inside to mend. Chuck couldn't believe his ears when he heard the dork say they had found the house keys and the USB stick inside the bird thing. SHIT. He had been looking at the booty for hours and didn't know it. They'd been told inside the house, not out in the damned garden. No matter, he was taking it to the station, which must be the local sheriff's office, so time to follow and retrieve. Limey police weren't armed, and the dork had no idea how important the USB stick was, so he assumed it would be like taking candy from a baby.

He ran down his escape route at the back of the garden and saw the car come out of the drive and head for the road opposite. Good, there were speed bumps up there and that would give him time to catch up. He sprinted to his car and set off in pursuit.

'Alpha, we have visual. Grey Mondeo saloon, one male occupant just entering cross roads.'

'Copy. Grey Mondeo. Single male. I will be turning right at end of road, then left at T-junction towards heath.'

'Alpha, copy that, right then left, we are 200 yards behind Mondeo.'

'I have visual… turning right... 200 yards to left turn.'

'Mondeo turning right… we are closing up.'
'Turning left, no more visual.'
'We have visual… Mondeo approaching junction… Turning left'
'I have visual…400 yards back…close up now.'

Terry could see the Mondeo accelerating towards him, so he began to slow down gradually to give the others a chance to catch up and close the trap. He saw them come round the corner about 150 yards behind the Mondeo, so he reached across to his bag and pulled out some tyre shredders and threw them out of the sunshine roof and onto the road behind him. As the Mondeo hit the shredders he hit the brakes and pulled the car into a broadside skid. Almost before the car had come to a stop he was out of the door and rolling behind the front wheels lining up a shot on the windscreen. His colleagues had completed the trap behind and were calling through a loudhailer.

'Armed police, Throw your weapons out of the car and then come out of the car with your hands up.'

The reply was a volley of gunfire into Terry's car, to which he replied with a couple of carefully placed shots. The first one was an armour piercing shell and went through the radiator into the engine block, the second one made a large hole in the windscreen next to where he though the driver's head would be. Meanwhile his colleagues took out the remaining two tyres, which hadn't been shredded yet.

'Armed police, Throw your weapons out of the car and then come out of the car with your hands up.'

This time, the driver's door started to open, so Terry

put a couple of shots into it so that the gunman would understand that he couldn't get out until his weapons had been thrown out. There was a pause of about thirty seconds and then a voice called out.

'OK, I'm throwing out my guns, don't shoot.' A handgun and a machine pistol were thrown from the car window and then the door slowly opened. The driver climbed out carefully with his hands over his head.

'Move away from the car towards me. Lie down on the ground and put your hands behind your back.'

With great care they approached the gunman, with one of them keeping out of range and constantly covering him. The second officer ensured that he didn't get in the firing line of Terry or his colleague and warily approached the gunman from the rear. Just as he was getting close, Terry saw the gunman bunch his muscles and start moving his arms, so he put a shot into the road next to his head. The gunman looked round towards him with surprise in his eyes and flopped to the ground in defeat, where he was quickly cuffed.

Terry walked up to the prisoner and studied his face carefully so that he could describe him to Angela.

'You really should give up smoking, you stink.'

Then he checked through the gunman's car and found a mobile phone, which he put in his pocket. Finally he nodded to his colleagues and turned back to his car, where he removed his balaclava as he drove back to the Professor's house.

'Who the fuck was that?' asked the prisoner, who

couldn't quite believe that the Brits had Rambo working for them.

'Bond, James Bond,' came the dry reply.

Chapter 34

Terry came back to the house in a somewhat battered car, loaded us all in and drove off at rapid speed. He explained that he wanted us back in the safe house as soon as possible, where he would fill us in on what had happened.

He took a few strange turns on the way back and having satisfied himself and Christine that no-one was following us he drove us into the safe house, where Edward was waiting for us with a worried expression.

'OK,' said Edward, 'we'll have a full debrief later, after which I can pass on all the relevant details to my colleagues, but I'd like to get the main points covered now please. Terry could you please describe the second gunman you and your colleagues took prisoner?'

Terry gave a very thorough description of the gunman and I confirmed that it indeed sounded exactly like one of the men from the cottage. He also handed over the mobile phone that he had taken from the gunman and Edward immediately organised for it to be taken away and analysed. Finally he explained that the only thing he could confirm about the man in the car chasing us was that he was large and black.

'Splendid, Terry, very well done. Angela, we will have pictures of the prisoner sent over for you to study, but if you are feeling strong enough, I believe you also have some good news for us?'

I told him about finding the USB stick and extracted it from my bra with a sheepish grin. We all marched off to the PC and a couple of minutes later we were waiting for WINDOWS to stir itself into life and reveal the contents of Dad's treasure. Jake went into Explorer and we looked at the list of files on the USB stick. There were only two files, one was called *Read_Me_First*, and the other was called *Instructions* so we started with the first one.

Congratulations, another step closer. No need to think diagonally now, just use Edward's name to unlock the other file.

'Who's Edward then?' asked Jake, 'a relation, a boyfriend, a teacher, or could he mean your real name Edward?'

'I don't think that would be the case as Angela's father never knew me as Edward – that is a name I made up just for this occasion, so I am afraid Angela is going to have to cast her mind further afield.'

'I don't know anyone called Edward,' I shook my

head, 'except John's teddy bear. Try the other file and see what it wants, and we can try Edward or Teddy, but that seems much too obvious.'

Jake tried both with no success, 'Sorry, no joy, any other ideas?'

'Well, I suppose we should try my teddy,' I looked at Jake daring him to laugh at my having a teddy, 'his name is Plank.' I could see they were all very surprised by my choice of name. 'Another old joke, what do you call a man with a plank on his head? Edward... Sorry Edward.'

Jake just shook his head in amused bewilderment and typed in Plank, whilst Edward said not to worry as it wasn't his name anyway.

Excellent!
Sorry to mislead you grunt_futtocks, but this USB stick does not contain the data you expected – but then you didn't really think that I would leave the details lying round for anyone to find, did you?
However, have no fear, what you are looking for is stored safely ready for release, and all you have to do is follow the instructions below exactly.
Option 1 – print this off and show it to me to prove you have cracked it all.
Option 2 – if I should be unavailable for any reason, go to the bank in Reigate and ask for Mr Cartwright, taking proof of your identity with you.

Fortunately I knew which bank Dad used, as he had set me up with an account there in preparation for

University. The only problem was that the Bank wouldn't be open again until Monday and my driving licence was burnt to ashes in the cottage, so we had come to a grinding halt. Edward said he would do his level best to see if he could find Mr Cartwright in the meantime, and asked where my passport was. I described to him exactly where my passport was in my bedroom as Edward was not allowing me anywhere near the house again. He said he would arrange for it to be collected and suggested that we had earned a day's rest, so we should just chill out and enjoy the facilities of the house.

Jake and I decided to go for a walk in the garden whilst Edward and Terry had a full debrief. We whistled to Mutt and Christine told us she would just wander along gently in the background. It was a joy to get some fresh air, but it was all very frustrating and we were desperate to move on to the next part, and to be honest it is not easy to relax when you realise that gunmen are actively trying to track you down.

Half an hour or so later, Christine called out to us and said we were wanted back in the house as the photos had come through. Right, action I thought, lead me on. I strode back to the house so fast that Jake was almost running to keep up with me, but it was worth it because Edward showed me a set of pictures and asked if I recognised anyone? One of the pictures showed the little shit who helped kill my parents and John and Susan. I almost smashed the screen as I pointed him out. Edward quietly stated that he would guarantee that he would never see the outside of a prison again, and apologised that the death penalty had been abolished. I just stared at the screen mouthing a string of obscenities until Jake gently led me away and reckoned that I needed a large glass of wine to calm me down.

Dinner was a strange affair. I wanted to quiz Terry about what had happened with the gunmen and he told me that he couldn't really tell me anything, just to be happy that two of them had been taken out of action and they were interrogating them now, which at least meant that DCI Jenkins was leaving me alone. Sod interrogation I thought, torture the little shits, but I wasn't sure they did that in the UK.

A short while later I decided I had had enough excitement for one day and went off to bed. The problem was that I just couldn't sleep, so when I heard Jake come up later, I was still wide awake and in need of some love and affection, and I was sure that Jake's head needed a check to see it wasn't still bleeding! I knocked on the door of his room and was very happy to hear his *come in*. He looked up and saw I was still wearing his old pyjamas, which made him grin. He grinned a lot more when I took them off, and suggested he might like checking out some more nooks and crannies. Yee- bloody-hah, Maslow was spot on!

Later on we lay next to one another and just talked and talked. It would appear that Christine was absolutely correct in her observation. Jake told me that he hadn't realised quite how much he missed me until I turned up in his life again, and he had been longing to let me know how he felt, but didn't want me to think he was taking advantage of me at the lowest point in my life. I told him that I had fancied him rotten for years, and that this stinking situation had at least come up with one good result. Dropping off to sleep in his arms was the best thing to have happened in days.

We were rather later than usual for breakfast the next morning, as it seemed silly to rush and there was someone between us who was fully awake, so we decided to not to waste any time in putting him to good use. Transpires the shower did have room for two.

When we eventually stumbled downstairs we met Christine in the dining room, who gave me a knowing look and a little grin, and I gave her a thumbs up behind Jake's back. She then pointed at the table and I saw my passport lying there, which she said had been delivered a short while before.

Edward had apparently had no luck in contacting Mr Cartwright, who appeared to be away for the weekend, so we had the rest of the day to ourselves, and she was sure we would find something to keep us amused. Fortunately Jake had enough condoms to last us until Monday! He had been rather embarrassed when I saw how many he had in his wash bag, and he told me he had stocked up for his relationship with Liz, but hadn't got round to using any of them as they had had an argument before he came to rescue me. More goodness, I thought as we had a lovely day in bed running down his supplies.

We met again in the evening for an update on the day's activities. Edward was alone as he said his colleagues were taking a day's rest and he would brief them in the morning. The bad news was that the prisoners were not talking yet, but they had made positive ids on them and they had been in prison at the same time as the big black guy. Unfortunately he hadn't been able to contact Mr Cartwright at all.

The only phone calls that had been made or received on the mobile phones that Jake had retrieved from the two killers were from one to the other and to one other number. The number, as Edward had expected, was a pay-as-you-go phone with no record of who owned it, but it was fair to guess that it belonged to the big black guy and he now knew that we had the USB stick. Ouch.

The other big news was a clip of video that he showed, which was taken from a CCTV in a motorway service station. The footage wasn't wonderful, but I would have recognised that big black bastard anywhere.

'Unfortunately, it doesn't get us very far as all it does is confirm that they were in the Range Rover you spotted on the way up the motorway, but we do now have pictures of Mr Brutus Carmichael circulated to all the police and security for next week's conference. I have also arranged for the news this evening to contain an item about two gangsters being unfortunately shot by the police after a car chase, and have thrown in some disinformation about a possible drug connection as I don't want our enemies to know we are on to them, and I certainly don't want them worrying about the loss of two of their number. That way I hope they think the USB stick is encrypted and we haven't managed to crack it yet.'

Edward paused and looked at me with a slightly hurt but expectant expression.

'Now, what we want to do is somehow capture the remaining gunman, and to do that I am afraid we are going to have to lure him out. What I propose we do is to announce just before the start of the conference that Angela will be speaking.'

There was pandemonium in the room as Jake argued that that would just set Angela up as a target and even Terry and Christine looked upset.

'STOP! Stop! There is, of course, no way I would put Angela's life in danger… let me tell you my plan.'

Chapter 35

I had put my sunglasses and baseball cap disguise back on when we entered the bank, as there was a slim chance that a neighbour could be down here shopping. Christine went up to the counter and asked if we could have a quiet word with Mr Cartwright, who transpired to be the manager. When asked who we were, she just said we were from the police and were simply looking for some help in tracing one of the bank's customers. A few minutes later Mr Cartwright appeared and Christine and I went through to his office whilst Jake and Terry stayed in the foyer with Mutt. Jake winked at me and suggested as there was a Boots next door that he would get some more *toothpaste*.

'So how can I help you officer? I hope none of our customers has been involved in some criminal activity?'

'No Sir,' replied Christine, 'nothing to worry about on that score. Can I ask you if you knew Professor

Harold Fenwick?'

Mr Cartwright nodded, and adopted a very sad expression, 'Yes, the Professor was a trusted customer of the bank, and I knew him well – is this about the tragic deaths of the Professor and his family?'

Christine looked across at me to check I was all right, and looked back at Mr Cartwright. 'Yes, indeed, Sir this is all to do with that tragedy. Before I continue I need to stress that this conversation is in total confidence and nothing is to be shared with anyone outside this room – not even another employee of the Bank.'

Mr Cartwright looked somewhat surprised, but confirmed that he was used to keeping customer confidences, and looked at us with an enquiring look on his face.

'Mr Cartwright, we believe the Professor left some instructions to be followed if you were approached by either his son or his daughter?'

'Indeed, there are instructions to that effect and I must admit I am in a slight quandary as to what to do with them in the circumstances. In fact, I have a meeting with the Professor's solicitor next week to discuss the matter as there appears to be no mention of the *instructions* in the will.'

'Well Sir, we can solve one problem for you, but as I said before I am afraid you cannot share this with anyone, even the family solicitor for the moment.'

Mr Cartwright was now looking thoroughly confused as Christine indicated that I should continue the conversation.

'Mr Cartwright, to steal a quote - *Reports of my death are greatly exaggerated* – I am Angela Fenwick, Professor Fenwick's daughter.' Mr Cartwright's jaw dropped a mile. 'To cut a long story short, my best friend died in the fire and I survived by sheer luck.'

'Oh, but that's wonderful news… oh sorry, that came out completely wrong … I mean I am enormously happy to see you have survived my dear, but I am very, very sorry about what happened to your friend and family.' I could see him struggling with a range of emotions, finally ending with confusion, 'but why is that a secret. We would have contacted you much earlier if we had known you were alive?'

Christine leant forwards and made sure she had Mr Cartwright's undivided attention. 'What hasn't been made public, Mr Cartwright, is the fact that Angela's family and friend were murdered and if the murderers knew that Angela was still alive, then her life would be in extreme danger.'

I could see that Mr Cartwright wanted to ask a whole set of questions, but Christine told him that it was best that he knew nothing else at this stage and to simply remember that NO-ONE was to hear about this conversation. Having recovered his composure, he then asked us to wait for a short while whilst he looked up my father's instructions in his files.

A couple of minutes later he turned to Christine and apologised, 'I'm very sorry, but I will have to ask you to leave the room as my instructions are that this information is only to be shared with the Professor's son or daughter.'

Christine didn't look happy, but she couldn't really refuse. I told her I would be fine and she said she would be just outside the door. Once she had left I turned back to Mr Cartwright and he started to read out the instructions that Dad had prepared.

'Firstly, I would like to see some proof of identity,' and I passed across my passport, which he carefully scrutinised.

'Secondly, who was Rocky?'

'My pony,' I replied. Ah, Dad really was being careful.

'Thirdly, what was fractured?'

'My brother's watch face.' I was almost enjoying this.

'Fourthly, what do you plan to do with the money you make from the information you hope to receive?'

'Sorry, I don't plan to make any money from it – Dad wanted everyone to have it for free?' That's why the bastards murdered him is what I thought and I certainly wasn't going to allow them to get away with it.

'Excellent, that is the answer he wanted, thank you. And finally what six numbers mean *it could be you*?'

'Sorry, that's thrown me. Could you repeat that?'

'What six numbers mean *it could be you*?'

'That's the second time he says *it could be you…*' I said thinking aloud. DOH, got it. 'Which is the phrase from the National Lottery from memory, so how about 5, 12, 17, 28, 30, 42?' which were the family Lottery numbers, based on our birthdays, our house number and 42 from *The Hitchhiker's Guide,* one of Dad's favourite books.

I waited with bated breath as Mr Cartwright checked the sequence I had given him on his PC to see if 42 and the other numbers really were the answer to everything.

'Excellent, I apologise for that, but your father wanted to be sure that the only people to progress from this point were you or your brother. Your father was a very cautious man, and I know he wanted to ensure that this information did not get into the wrong hands, so do not be upset when I tell you that you will not be taking anything away with you this afternoon, as he wanted to also be sure that you had not been forced into coming here against your own free will… I know, please bear with me…Unfortunately your father had not reckoned with the ruthlessness of the world out there, but I think when you hear what he planned you will be more than happy.'

A few minutes later I came out shaking my head at the way my Dad's brain worked and joined the others. They looked very surprised when they saw I was carrying nothing, but I assured them that everything was all right. I grabbed Mutt's lead and Jake's hand and asked him if he had managed to get his toothpaste. A big tube, he was happy to report.

Chapter 36

To say the atmosphere on the 'phone between Brutus and the Sheikh was frosty would be the understatement of the year. Brutus had not been looking forwards to the call, but decided in the end that the Sheikh was such a good source of income that he had to take his punishment like a man and not like some little frightened punk. So when his 'phone rang and the Sheikh spoke to him, it was almost a relief.

'Mr Carmichael, I do not pay you exorbitant sums of money to have your colleagues plastered all over the evening news....DO NOT INTERRUPT ME...The only good news that I can see, in spite of your gross incompetence, is that the police think the whole episode is related to drugs and they haven't worked out the contents of the USB stick yet.' The Sheikh paused for a moment, and Brutus was at least sensible enough to keep quiet. 'Coming as you do from a cultural backwater, you are probably too ignorant to know the works of Oscar Wilde, so let me paraphrase one of his most famous sayings for you - *to lose one colleague, Mr Carmichael, may be regarded as a misfortune; to lose both looks like carelessness* - I do not tolerate carelessness Mr Carmichael. Find that stick and destroy it or I will destroy you. Have a nice day.'

Oh he would find it, and he would rip anyone to shreds who got in his way. This plan kept going wrong too many times and it was time to get it back the way he liked it. Not just for that shit, the Sheikh; he needed to guarantee his secret payment from the oil company CEO as well.

Part 3 - Showtime

Chapter 37

The monitoring van was stacked full of equipment with feeds from the cameras all over the conference centre. It was a little crowded as Jake and I were in there together with Edward and his American colleague Charles and there were a couple of technicians as well. Jake and I had been smuggled in early in the morning and were now constantly checking the monitors for any sign of the Big Black Bastard, or *triple B* as I now called him.

The agenda for the conference now had a special slot in the middle of the morning, entitled *A Tribute to Professor Harold Fenwick,* and the speaker names were listed as William and Jake Barton, followed by Angela Fenwick. Jake and his Dad refused to let me go on stage by myself, and had also quite reasonably stated that Dad had been a very close friend and they wanted to pay their respects as well. Edward was convinced that having my name on there was going to draw out *triple B* as the gunman firstly had no idea I knew what he looked like, and secondly couldn't ignore the possibility of my having access to Dad's work. All of which convinced Edward that *triple B* would make an attempt to find out what I knew.

Fortunately the combination of being black and large narrowed down the search, but as this was a major International conference, there were people of all shapes and colours and certainly many large black people. What we weren't sure about was whether he would sit in the audience and wait to see what happened in my speech, or take the risk of trying to find me backstage beforehand. Edward's gut reaction was he would try to get backstage, so I was concentrating on the monitors showing those areas.

'There...just a minute, how do I zoom this one? Thanks, that's better, yes, yes, that's *triple B*!'

Even though I knew there were a hundred yards and numerous policemen between me and the murdering bastard, I was shrinking back into the corner and clutching Jake's hand for dear life. Now we needed Edward's plan to work and no-one to get hurt.

Triple B had dressed himself as a security guard so as not to stand out, and Edward had instructed the checkpoints to let him through, as he didn't want any dead heroes. We watched his progress on the monitor screens as he worked his way towards the dressing rooms, as Edward and the technicians fed information to Terry and the others. Finding the door marked with Barton/Fenwick he was just about to knock and enter, when David Hall came round the corner limping heavily with his walking stick and saying that he was

Mr Barton and asking if he could help.

'Just coming to check everything is all right with you and Miss Fenwick, Sir.'

'Most kind, most kind, do go in,' replied Mr Hall, and just as he said that the dressing room door began to open and *triple B* couldn't resist taking a quick glance that way. It was more than enough time for Mr Hall to raise his stick and press the gas release button. A dart flew out of the end into *triple B*'s thigh and he stumbled through the door with a look of disbelief on his face as he tried to reach for his pistol. He could see the Professor's daughter sitting in front of the mirror, with the USB stick lying next to her, but he couldn't get his legs to move properly. The next thing he knew was total blackness as something heavy hit the back of his head.

'Slight overkill possibly David, as that dart of yours seems to be doing the trick, but they told me not to trust the bastard, and to be honest I think Angela would have liked me to hit him even harder!' was Terry's comment as he made sure that *triple B* was securely cuffed at wrist and ankle.

Christine turned round from the mirror and started to remove her wig and Kevlar jacket.

'Can't say I enjoyed that. I was ready to shoot him the moment he walked in, but Edward did tell us to try and keep him alive. Well done, David, a neat little device.'

'Yes, not sure I'll be allowed to keep it, now they know I have it, but it throws people when they see someone limping, makes you look harmless.'

At that moment several police officers arrived followed by Edward and Charles. Jake and I were bringing up the rear with another couple of policemen, waiting to hear it was safe. They had wanted me to stay in the van, but there was no way I was going to miss the chance of looking my father's killer in the eye. Edward checked the situation and turned back to me, indicating that it was safe to come forwards.

'Can you roll him over? Is that safe? Only I want to see his face please?'

Terry and David were convinced he was out cold, but they continued to cover him whilst two officers rolled him over.

'He's out cold?' I asked, and they nodded. 'Shame,' I said as I lifted my foot and drove it straight into his testicles. 'Sorry, lost my footing?' People were looking slightly taken aback, but Edward said he had no idea what I was talking about and had seen nothing.

'Right, let's get out there and wow them, shall we?'

The three of us marched off towards the stage and an audience that I hoped would be very surprised by what I had to say, whilst Edward said he would watch the action from backstage with his American colleague.

Round the corner, well away from the dressing room that Terry and Christine had used for the trap was another room guarded by a colleague of Terry, who opened the door as we approached. Inside, waiting for news was Uncle Bill and to my surprise and delight Susan's parents. I ran across the room and fell into Susan's Mum's arms and we just stood there not saying a word for a while. I tried to apologise, but they just told me to not be silly, none of it was my fault, and if they understood right, the whole thing would be sorted out in the next few minutes. I thanked them profusely for helping keep the secret, and they assured me it was what Susan would have wanted, and then I told them the good news that all three gunmen had now been captured and would be rotting away in jail for the rest of their despicable lives.

Uncle Bill came over to us and gently tapped me on the shoulder and said he was sorry, but we had to go on stage now. Susan's parents said they would be out front listening.

Chapter 38

'I first met Harold Fenwick twenty years ago, when we were neighbours down in Surrey. I had little idea at that time that we were destined to become extremely close friends and also mutually beneficial business colleagues. Harold, as some of you know, had a huge intellect tied to that rare breed of person, who wants to improve the world for his fellow human beings. Yes, I will admit that we both profited from his inventions, with Harold providing the brains and me providing the financial backing, but he never came to me with an idea that was exclusively for his own benefit. No, the overriding concern was whether it would help other people and especially his number one concern – this fragile planet that we live on, which is why Harold's untimely death is such a tragic loss, not only to his family and friends but also to each and every one of you.' Uncle Bill paused for a moment. 'Now, I would like to hand you over to my son, who would like to say a few words.'

The cameras swung round to the second podium, where Jake was waiting for his cue from his Dad. He looked at me in the wings, gave me a wink and started his speech.

'Ladies and gentlemen, just over a week ago, Harold took his family for a holiday up in the Lake District. As you have no doubt seen in the media, there was a fire in the cottage where they were staying and four people died in the fire – Harold, his wife Gudrun, his son John and their daughter's best friend Susan Mortimer. Harold's daughter Angela would no doubt have died in the fire as well, but by sheer luck she was not in the cottage at the time.'

Jake stopped, smiled quickly at me and then looked at the audience, because he could hear confused murmurs.

'I am sure some of you are thinking that you heard in the media that the Professor's daughter was one of the people in the fire, and yet she is supposedly speaking today. I must apologise. You were intentionally misled about her death, because the fire was most certainly *not accidental*. NO, the Professor and the others were callously murdered by gunmen, who had come to steal the Professor's latest work.'

There were gasps from the audience, who were now riveted.

'How do I know this... well that's because there was an eye-witness to those tragic events, and to protect her life the police decided to feed out the disinformation that she had died in the fire. The good news is that the three thugs responsible for this hideous crime have now been arrested by the police, and hence it gives me great pleasure to introduce the survivor of that awful evening, Angela Fenwick.'

There were a few moments' silence, and then the audience erupted in a crashing round of applause as I took the stage. To be honest, I was absolutely terrified as I saw the sea of faces out there, but Jake whispered to me *naked*, to remind me of his advice to just pretend they were all sitting there naked, and that made me lose my nerves. Well almost.

'J,j,just before,' I cleared my throat and took a sip of water, 'just before my father died, he had come up with what he considered to be the most important invention of his life. As you have just heard, conservation of the planet was Dad's dream, and he wanted his invention to be used to achieve that aim and not, in his words, *get bogged down in politics and bureaucracy*.'

There were a few chuckles from the audience.

'Just before he died, my father told us that he had worked out how to produce an easily manufactured source of energy, which did not use fossil fuels, did not pollute the planet, and was incredibly cheap to run – for him the Holy Grail.'

That got a surprised gasp from the audience.

'That is what my father's murderers stole, and it's not really surprising as his invention must have been worth billions. However, those ruthless killers did not actually want it for themselves... no, their plan was to destroy my father's work and continue to milk the billions they could get from oil. Unfortunately I don't know who they were representing, or who was behind the whole thing, but I do know that to lose such an invention is a crying shame, as Dad told me it was very unlikely that anyone else would hit upon his idea, as it had frankly been a lucky mistake.'

That one got a loud groan, and I made a suitably sad face, but they didn't know what I had up my sleeve.

'Dad also loved Harry Potter, and for those of you who have read the first book, you will remember that only Harry could pull the ultimate prize – the Philosopher's Stone - out of his pocket as he didn't want it for himself. So Dad left me his Philosopher's Stone.'

OK, I thought, that's got their attention, now it's time to knock their socks off.

'Ladies and gentlemen, my father's invention did not die with him. In fact he left full details of it, which will be released to the world's media and Universities and websites as soon as I give the password...' you could have heard a pin drop, '... namely that the conditions that Dad wanted for his invention are... that it should be made available to every nation on earth WITH NO CONDITIONS WHATSOEVER AND AT NO COST.'

Behind me one screen started showing live footage from the safety deposit box, which the Bank would only open when I had said the invention was for everybody, not for me. The contents were extracted and then the second screen started showing Dad's working diagrams and instructions. The audience rose as one and started stamping and clapping like maniacs.

God, Dad, why aren't you here to see it? The tears were coming again, and Jake came across and led me off the stage to sit in peace and quiet and compose myself, whilst Uncle Bill started to field the avalanche of questions.

At the back of the auditorium, a very irate oil company CEO stormed out in a rage, with his phone stuck to his ear as he tried to reach his stockbroker.

Chapter 39

As we came off stage, Terry and Christine grabbed us and led us to a room where Charles was slumped in a chair looking as if he had had a severe shock. He didn't seem to take in who was coming and going and just sat their mumbling to himself *he's going to kill me, what can I do, hell*, when Edward walked up to him, slapped him round the face and told him that the only way out now was to help us.

'Allow me to explain,' Edward started, 'there have been simply too many strange coincidences in this whole affair. For instance, how did anyone know about the hydrogen storage for the fuel cell in the first place? How did they know to intercept the package going to your father's lawyers?'

Neither of us could answer, so he continued.

'I had your mother's mobile phone records analysed Angela, as I am sorry to say that I thought that was the only place where the leak could have started. Imagine my surprise to see a number come up that was very familiar to me.'

Edward looked across at Charles with a worried frown.

'I am afraid I have suspected for some time that there was a traitor in the ranks of the committee, so I set up some little tests for our friend here. Firstly, I couldn't help noticing that Charles found it incredibly difficult to look you in the eyes whenever he met you at the safe house.'

I nodded agreement, as I had wondered about that too.

'Secondly I ensured that he did not know about the meeting you set up with the American impostor in the pub. Only Andrew and I knew about that. The fact that that meeting and subsequent arrest went off without a hitch began to confirm my suspicions.'

Edward checked we were following along as he gritted his teeth and tried not to do Charles any further harm.

'Then today - did you notice how easily Brutus found your dressing room in this vast complex? I fed that information to Charles, but I failed to tell him that it was a trap. I also conveniently forgot to tell him that you did actually have your father's workings – Charles here thought they were safely stolen and passed on, which was going to guarantee him a large retirement fund if I am guessing correctly. You should have seen his face when you announced them to the world – shattered is a severe understatement.'

Edward looked at Charles with deep loathing and

leant closer to his face.

'Would you like to explain your treachery to Angela, you scum? Would you like to look her in the face and tell her that your treachery resulted in the death of her family just so you could line your pockets with some cash? No, I thought not.'

Edward was seething and obviously close to beating Charles to a pulp, but he managed to hold himself back.

'Charles, unfortunately, is an old hand at this game, so his phone records showed nothing untoward. I assume he carefully uses public telephones or throw-away mobiles to contact his paymaster. The only way, Charles, that you are getting out of this room in a healthy state is to tell us who your contact is and how to get hold of them.'

'But, he'll kill me,' Charles muttered.

'I can organise that if you wish, Charles – just walk out that door and I will broadcast your whereabouts. I am sure *the Sheikh* will find you very quickly and ask where it all went wrong. Or, tell me how to find him, and I will guarantee you will live to see another day. Which is it to be?'

Charles bent his head in abject shame and refused to look at me at all.

'I'm sorry, really truly sorry. I didn't want anyone to get hurt.' He looked up at me with pleading eyes. 'I honestly didn't think anyone would be harmed, I was just trying to get your mother the best deal. You must believe me?'

Oh I believed the stupid, lying, two-faced bastard as

I spat in his face and left the room.

Chapter 40

The Sheikh and his brother had been watching the news coverage of the conference. When the Professor's daughter took to the stage, they realised that Brutus had obviously failed in his mission, however as she started to speak it sounded just like a tribute to her father and nothing to worry about. Then she dropped the bombshell of her father's work being available to everybody for nothing and the Sheikh nearly threw the television out of the window. All that effort for nothing. The Professor must have hidden another copy on the USB stick, and the daughter had been able to follow the trail and find it. 'What shall we do with the girl?'

'Leave her,' replied the Sheikh, 'killing her is unnecessary, and will attract unwelcome attention. Instead we will let her spend the rest of her life looking over her shoulder wondering when we are going to exact our revenge. Now, as there appears to be nothing left for us in this miserable country, I will tell the charter company to have the jet ready to leave as soon as possible.'

Whilst they were packing everything ready to leave, there was a phone call from the charter company apologising that there was a minor technical fault on the jet. It was being fixed as fast as possible, but it meant a short delay.

Rather than get upset, the Sheikh and his brother decided to have a final good lunch with some excellent wine. The phone rang just as they were finishing to say the jet was ready to roll, so a short while later the Sheikh and his brother were being driven to the airfield, where the jet was waiting. Five minutes later, they were seated on board and enjoying a glass of champagne prior to take-off, served by a very attentive steward. Fortunately neither of them noticed the slightly strange taste, but panic only began to set in after about two minutes, when they both noticed that they couldn't move their arms or legs.

'Good evening, Hashim and Mansur, I believe. I wouldn't try moving if I were you, the drug in your champagne is a very powerful muscle relaxant, which means you can hear me, but you can't move at all – rather useful I find for this sort of occasion. My American colleague, known to you as *cell-out*, sends his regards, and would have been here to see you off, but he had rather an unfortunate accident, such a shame. Anyway, do enjoy your flight, although the destination is not quite what you had in mind. They tell me that Guantanamo Bay is delightful this time of year,' and with that Edward left the aircraft and waved to them as they taxied off to incarceration.

Chapter 41

The next few weeks were a whirlwind. Jake and his Dad were absolute stalwarts as they organised one thing after another for me, because the media were constantly clamouring for *exclusive* interviews. I turned all of them down as I had no interest whatsoever in making money from the death of my family – that just struck me as bizarre and unhealthy.

However, I did agree to appear on one chat show on TV as I thought that was the quickest way to get the correct story out there. I even got invited to tea with the Prime Minister, but as Dad had hated him and thought him to be an *incompetent thieving git*, it struck me as somewhat hypocritical to accept the invitation.

Edward was brilliant as he also allowed us to carry on using the safe house until everything was sorted. I was then going to move up to Cheshire and live with the Bartons until I got my life sorted out, as I had no desire to rattle round in our old house all by myself.

Jake and I are looking to see if I can get into Leeds, so that I will be with him when the year starts again at Uni.

The stock-markets obviously had a major reaction to the news that the world was not going to be totally dependent on fossils fuels any more, and Edward came past one evening to give me two great pieces of news. Firstly, they had managed to freeze a large part of the Sheikh's money that he was planning to suck out of the markets, and secondly they had secured an agreement that the three gunmen would be extradited to the US to face charges over there. I couldn't quite see the advantage of that until Edward explained to me that Brutus definitely, and the others probably, were wanted for murder in the US and they would face the death penalty if found guilty.

He also told me that Brutus was still suffering from groin pain, which made me happier still. Once the three of them had heard that the Sheikh was in captivity, they had started spilling all the details they could in an attempt to reduce their sentence, but Edward was convinced that wasn't going to save them. DCI Jenkins also rang up and apologised, which I thought was good of him as he had really only been doing his job, and my actions were probably not all that rational in retrospect.

We arranged a very quiet cremation for Mum, Dad and John as I hate funerals and I didn't really want loads of people there. Then I took their ashes up to the top of Lady Hill and let them drift gently away on the wind next to a bench that Mum and Dad used to love to sit on and admire the view, which was also about half way between *Fracture* and *Rocky*, and that seemed somehow rather apt.

Uncle Bill organised a memorial service at our local church in the village for them and Susan, whose funeral was also quiet and private to avoid the media, and I don't think I have ever seen the place so full. People from all sorts of backgrounds were coming up and shaking my hand, and most of it passed in a daze to be honest, but I do remember one particular chap who winked at me and said *well done grunt_futtock* in a voice I had last heard down the phone. Then he disappeared very quickly and I saw Terry drive him away.

When the circus had died down and the memorial service was over I went out with Jake and Mutt, and we paid what I thought was a final fitting tribute to Dad. We took the little film canisters back to the old car wreck and the blasted tree and replaced them, which I must admit very nearly had me in tears again. Then we went back to the house and fired up the *grunt_futtock* id on geocaching and amended the cache pages, so that anyone could have the fun of trying to solve the puzzles and find the caches.

Bet you *Got2Bfirst* gets the FTF!

Author's note

I must admit that I do not know whether hydrogen fuel cells are the answer to this planet's energy problems, but I am convinced that fossil fuels will soon run out, and we desperately need something pollution-free to replace them. This may be nuclear fusion, solar / tidal / wind power or whatever. There are numerous websites out there, which you can peruse, which argue the various cases – one will tell you that fuel cells are the future, the next will tell you that hydrogen is a waste of time and money. Pass.

The actual device the Professor invents is not that important; the implications of someone coming up with a viable alternative to fossil fuels, however, are enormous and that is what I wanted to get people thinking about. Try entering Peak Oil in Google and see where it takes you.

The two *grunt_futtock* caches *About Time*, and *There's no F in Greece* are available on the geocaching website. They were published during the writing of the book in order to test out parts of the story line and to see if they could be solved with the addition of "normal" clues. They have both been found by the local geocaching gurus, some using the book and some without.

The final cache, leading to the location of the keys and the USB stick does not actually use the coordinates of my house for obvious reasons. The coordinates were, in fact, for one of my caches, called *Our first bonus cache,* but I have had to move that cache recently so I am afraid you will have to either hunt around nearby or solve the puzzles for that one! The idea for the hiding place for the keys, though, does come from a local cache, but I won't say which one as that would give the game away. Another cache published by *parmstro and grunt_futtock* uses the DA puzzle scheme in the book.

Membership of the geocaching community is absolutely free, you just need to register on the www.geocaching.com website.